LEATHER BOYS

Book 4 of the Men in Motion Series

BY G.A. HAUSER

LEATHER BOYS
Book Four of the Men in Motion Series
Copyright © G.A. HAUSER, 2010
Cover art by Stephanie Vaughan
Trade Paperback ISBN: 978-1449-5928-3-7

The GA Hauser Collection

Second printing The GA Hauser Collection July 2010

WARNING

This book contains material that maybe offensive to some:

graphic language, homosexual relations, adult situations.

Please store your books carefully where they cannot be

accessed by underage readers.

Chapter One

Devlin Young had known about the Sturgis motorcycle gathering since he was ten. His father, Jan, used to own a Harley Davidson chopper. Every year in August Jan would take off on a wild ride to that colossal bikers' extravaganza with Dev's mother, Melinda, on the back of his roadster. The year Dev turned thirteen he was finally old enough to join them, riding along in a sidecar. They continued to go as a family for the next three years until Jan had an accident at work and was unable to ride the bike any longer. Fourteen years later, Dev was about to return to the madness of the event. And he couldn't wait.

As Dev polished his brand new Kawasaki, making the chrome gleam like a mirror, he smiled contentedly. "That's yet another good thing to come out of my divorce," he muttered, crouched down in his garage in Centerville, Ohio, rubbing his "baby" down before he rode to the club meeting.

Standing back, finally satisfied she didn't have a fingerprint on her, Dev made sure he had everything he needed. Wearing his black leather jacket and a pair of jeans, he placed his helmet on his head and straddled the seat with as much excitement as if he were mounting a lover. Priming it, pushing in the choke, he turned the key in the ignition, loving the sound and vibration under his ass. Dev drove out of the garage, clicking the remote to close it as he accelerated out of his quiet condominium complex.

Ten minutes later, he pulled into the parking lot of the Kettering Bar and Grille. Counting almost a dozen motorcycles already out front, Dev felt his pulse race. Propping the bike up on its kickstand, he removed his helmet and hurried inside. In anticipation of meeting everyone face to face, he pushed back the front door to the bar. It was the first gathering he had attended, but he had spoken to Jerry Macy over the phone. Jerry ran the club, organizing the meetings and a few other group events, including Sturgis, throughout the year.

Seeing a large table cluttered with enamel helmets, Dev knew he was in the right room. Upon entering, some of the group members noticed him and looked up.

"Hey." He waved shyly. "I'm Devlin Young. I spoke to Jerry last week about joining."

A man in his fifties with gray peppering his black hair acknowledged him. "Devlin, welcome aboard." As he made introductions around the room, Dev knew the names would go right through him. He was terrible at remembering them.

A young man sitting near a vacant seat coaxed him over.

Placing his helmet on the table with all the others, like a trophy of their beloved sport, Dev asked, "Am I late?"

"No. Not at all. We don't usually start 'til eight."

"I'm sorry. Jerry went around the circle so quickly I didn't get your name."

"Sam. Sam Rhodes."

"Sam." Dev shook his hand. After admiring Sam's good looks for a moment, Dev tuned back in to Jerry's instructions.

"We could meet up here, or at my place. I don't see any problem with either," Jerry announced. "I'm also open to suggestions."

A man with dark black hair, a finely trimmed goatee, and a tattoo of an eagle on his shoulder asked, "What's wrong with a lot close to Interstate 675? I wouldn't mind hitting the Cracker Barrel on Wilmington Pike for breakfast first, then we have freeway access right out the door."

"Sounds good. Anyone else other than Tony have a suggestion?" Jerry eyed the members in the room.

Dev tried to commit their names to his memory. Tony, the dark-haired guy with the eagle tattoo. Jerry, middle-aged fellow, graying hair. *What was that other guy's name? Doug?*

Most of the members were older than he had expected. Out of the dozen attendees, only three or four seemed to be under or around thirty. The rest were obviously fifty-plus. He hated to admit he preferred it that way. He'd seen what young men in their early twenties were like in organizing an event. They sucked.

"Since we have several new members joining us tonight, why don't we go around the room and just say a little about ourselves." Jerry added. "I can begin. I'm Jerry Macy, head of this wonderful motorcycle group called the Leather Boys. I'm married to my lovely wife, June." He gestured to a sweet looking middle-aged lady sitting next to him. "We've got two grown kids and I own a printing business in Sugarcreek."

As each member spoke about themselves, Dev paid closer attention to the ones who seemed more interesting. The dark-haired, tattooed man had a wicked smile. "Yeah, I'm Tony Spagna, originally from New York. I'm thirty, married, I work as a teacher for Fairborn elementary school."

3

"Hi, everyone. I'm Ralph Jacobs. I'm married to Kay," he touched the pretty woman next to him on the shoulder, "and we have two small children, three and five. I work as a mechanic for Planet Ford."

Dev lost interest in some of the long-winded speakers. It was just a hello for crying out loud, not a speech. There was Douglas Allen, the divorced fifty-year-old ex-marine who worked security at the courthouse downtown, and a few older, balding, gray-haired men who completely lost Dev's attention as they rambled on about how wonderful their businesses were and everyone should patronize them.

Next was Sam, who perked Dev's attention back up.

"Hi, to all you newcomers. As I am relatively new myself. I'm Sam Rhodes, twenty-eight, single, and live in Centerville. I have my own business as a web designer and host and I'm happy to be part of the group."

Dev found all eyes on him. He cleared his throat. "I'm Devlin, or Dev Young, thirty, divorced, no kids, I'm self-employed as a writer..." He noticed he had piqued Sam's interest instantly. "And I'm just glad to be here and to be going to Sturgis with all of you."

Jerry smiled and tried to be heard over the chatter. "Right. August fifth, everyone will meet at the Cracker Barrel on Wilmington Pike for breakfast. Early. It has to be about seven in the morning, people. Then we'll hit I675 and head out to South Dakota. Any questions before we have beer and food?"

As the noise level grew, Sam leaned closer to Dev to ask, "What do you write?"

"Fiction. So? Web designer?"

"Yes. Do you have an author website?"

"No. Not yet."

"I can help you with one."

"I should. I know it's your calling card on the net."

"Have you published anything? What kind of books do you write?"

Dev was embarrassed to tell Sam what he wrote. Not many people were big fans of his genre, so he usually lied about their content. "I've published quite a few. Uh, thrillers, mystery, you know." A waitress arrived to take orders for their drinks and food.

Listening to Sam order a beer and burger, Dev said, "The same," when the waitress asked him.

"Have you ever been to Sturgis?"

"Yes. Many moons ago. My dad is a big fan of motorcycles." Dev loved the way Sam's hair color matched his eyes, both the exact same shade of chocolate brown. Delightful.

"I've never been there. It's like the place is legendary for Harley riders. I bet I get a lot of grief for riding a Japanese bike."

"Nah, I talked to my dad about it. There are plenty of Japanese and Italian bikes there now. The main thing is you have to ride there. If you show up with a truck and trailer you're dead meat." Dev laughed and noticed Tony trying to listen from across the table. "What do you drive, Tony?" Dev asked, attempting to involve him.

"Harley Sportster."

"Oh, you'll have no problem fitting in."

"I used to own a Ducati. But I traded it in."

Sam shouted, "Why don't you move down to our end of the table?"

Dev looked across from him at the few vacant seats. It appeared the older crowd knew each other so well they were like bar buddies and inevitably cliques began to form.

As Tony stood and relocated to be closer to them, Dev admired his tightly packed body. Though Tony wasn't tall he seemed very powerful.

When Tony was sitting across from Sam and him, Dev asked, "Are we the only young guys?"

"Ralph is in his thirties." Tony pointed to the bearded man who had stated he was a mechanic.

"That's right." Dev nodded.

Their beers were placed before them.

As the waitress set his down, Dev watched the foam float over the side of the glass slowly, like in an advertisement for alcohol.

"I assume we're all staying at Buffalo Chip campgrounds." Tony sipped his ale.

Sam replied, "Yes. That was the plan. I heard if you bring a tent it's first come first serve."

As he listened, Dev allowed his glass to drip on the table before he brought it to his lips and got it all over his shirt.

"We can camp together. It'll be great." Sam smiled brightly at Dev.

Dev lit up at his adorable dimples. "I'd like that."

"I wonder what the hell it'll be like." Tony leaned his elbows on the table

Dev took a sip of his beer. "I've been there. I remember my dad had an attitude that the bikers did what the fuck they pleased. There isn't a lot the locals can do about it."

Tony smiled. "Can you imagine the cops dealing with that crowd?"

"Exactly."

Sam smiled at Dev. "Man, I'm going to like hanging with you. You're a tough boy, aren't you?"

Choking on his beer, Dev laughed. "Me? Uh, you're describing my dad, not me." Dev looked over at Tony who was staring at him. Pointing to Tony, Dev said to Sam, "He's the tough one. Look at his damn tattoo."

"I've got one." Sam yanked his shirt up over his chest, pulling his right arm out of the sleeve.

Dev almost passed out at the sight of his incredibly ripped torso. Twisting in his chair, Sam showed off his small tattoo on his left shoulder blade.

"What the hell is it?" Tony leaned over the table to look.

"It's a dragon. Can't you tell?"

Dev covered his mouth. Sam was so damn delectable he couldn't stand it.

"A dragon? That little thing?" Tony teased. "Ya gotta show your patriotism, men." Tony rolled his short-sleeved T-shirt up to expose his entire tattoo. Adding to the power, he flexed his biceps.

Dev wanted to stroke that solid muscle in admiration. "Very impressive. A Harley and an eagle tattoo. That's the perfect combination for success at Sturgis, believe me."

As he rolled the sleeve back down and Sam straightened his shirt, Tony announced, "I'm planning on getting a nice piece of ass while I'm there. I hear the biker chicks are wild."

Sam tilted his head. "Aren't you married?"

"In theory."

Dev laughed. "In theory? What the fuck does that mean?"

"Look. I am married, but I wouldn't mind a little on the side."

"Does your wife know that?" Sam asked in amazement.

"No! What are you, stupid?"

Two plates with a burger and fries appeared. Dev sat back as the waitress put them down.

Trying to be polite, Dev waited until Tony got his. "You did order, didn't you?" he asked.

Tony nodded. "Yeah. Same thing."

"Have a fry." Dev pushed his plate across to him.

Taking one, Tony chewed it, saying, "Thanks."

Before he ate, Dev noticed Sam stretching over the table to ask Jerry something. Waiting to figure out what he was up to, Dev ate a few of his french fries.

Jerry passed a piece of paper to Sam. "Here's the pamphlet for events that are taking place at the campsite."

Sam read it over. "Maybe we should exchange mobile phone numbers or something."

"I thought that was what Jerry was going to do," Tony replied. "Wasn't he getting us all a list to take home?"

Sam leaned closer to their little trio so he wouldn't be overheard. "I think he's really just concerned with his old cronies."

"I hate that shit," Tony sneered, looking back at the other men.

"Well," Sam replied, "they've been in the group for ages. Only us younger guys are new at it."

Dev finished chewing and added, "There aren't many groups around this area. Locally, I mean. There are in downtown Dayton, and a few in Cincinnati and Columbus, but nothing really in Greene or Montgomery County."

"I know," Tony agreed. "I found the same thing."

"Look, screw them." Dev sipped his beer. "We'll ride up with them as a group and go off on our own if we want to."

"What about Ralph?" Sam indicated him with a tilt of his head.

"I don't mind if he hangs around with us." Dev checked him out again. "But he seems more than happy to associate with the older generation."

"I'll ask him later. In private," Tony assured. "You two are lucky you're both single." He ate the last bite of his hamburger, wiping his hands on a napkin.

"Can I ask why you're married?" Dev ate another fry.

"Long story. Maybe at Sturgis, over a beer. No make that over a few beers." Tony rolled his eyes.

"I was married for seven years, but lived with my ex for ten. She never let me ride to this event, with or without her." Dev finished eating, pushing the plate aside.

"Is that why you divorced?" Sam asked.

"One of the reasons." Dev winked at him loving the blush in Sam's cheeks in response. *Oh, you hot fucker you...*

"I should get a divorce," Tony moaned. "It's just that both our families are strict Catholics. The pressure's really on to stay together."

"Any kids?" Sam asked, setting his empty plate on top of Dev's.

"No. Thank fuck. I use condoms even though she thinks it's a fucking sin. I get overdosed with kids all day at my job. By the time I get home I've had more than enough screaming for the day."

"I can't picture you teaching elementary school." Dev finished his beer.

"Why?"

"I don't know. You look like a tough New Yorker."

"I am a tough New Yorker. What the hell do you think? I beat the kids up?" he laughed.

"You must scare the crap out of them."

"No. Nothing like that. They love me."

Dev exchanged grins with Sam at Tony's boasting. "Bet they're scared shitless."

As Sam broke up with laughter, Dev imagined wrapping around Sam for a cuddle. He was so turned on by the handsome man he wondered what would happen at Sturgis. In the mass of crazy drunk and stoned men in leather, could he entice him for some erotic fun? Time would tell.

Jerry Macy's booming voice tried to quiet the group. "I have some maps I've printed up." He handed a pile to pass around. "It's a no-brainer. Interstate 75 to 90. We can take 90 right into Rapid City. It's around twelve hundred and seventy-five miles, so we'll take plenty of rest stops along the way for our sore butt cheeks. And we'll stop on the way up overnight in Sioux Falls. There's a KOA close by the highway. I wasn't planning a stop for the way back. I'll leave it up to the individual."

Sam looked back at Dev with a smile.

"I don't have all your itineraries, but I expect once we get there we'll all go to the campground. I've also listed some mobile phone numbers." He produced another paper, "If you find yours is missing, write your number on it. Pass it around, Ralph. I'll photocopy all of it and hand it out when we meet up for breakfast. That way, if you want to gather as a group, we can arrange it even if we're all in different places."

Tony leaned across the table. "At least he's got it covered now. Better late than never."

Dev shrugged.

The paper made its way to their end of the table. Dev leaned over Sam's shoulder to watch him write his number down. When Sam handed him the paper, Dev repeated Sam's number to get it into his head and commit to memory. As he wrote his, he noticed Sam staring, possibly doing the same thing. Deciding on going for it, after Dev handed Tony the paper, he said, "Let me give you mine." Dev took a clean paper napkin and scribbled his home and mobile phone number down, handing it to Sam.

Reaching for Dev's pen, Sam reciprocated.

"You want mine?" Tony asked as he passed the number list to Doug.

Being polite, Dev pushed the napkin toward him, handing him a pen.

"Looks like it's us three," Sam mused out loud.

"It's easier that way," Dev commented. "I've been there before. Trying to please twenty people and make a command decision is murder. Being in a small group is a hell of a lot easier."

Tony handed Dev his napkin and took Sam's to write his phone number on his.

Once the three of them had exchanged their info, Dev looked back up to Jerry to see if the meeting was over.

"Anyone riding in the mayor's ride?" Jerry asked.

No one raised their hands.

Acknowledging it, Jerry said, "I know. It's expensive. I didn't do it either. Right. Any questions?" No one spoke up. "All right. I'll see you all Tuesday the fifth at seven sharp. If you're not there, we'll leave without you."

"Ooh." Tony rolled his eyes at the threat.

"That's it. See ya Tuesday." Jerry adjourned the meeting.

No one stood to go. Dev leaned closer to Sam to ask, "I take it we don't have any dorky patch or insignia to wear to show we're a group."

"Jerry made up T-shirts. Didn't you get one?" Sam asked.

"No."

"Jerry!" Sam shouted. "Dev didn't get a shirt!"

"What size?" Jerry shouted back.

"Large!" Dev yelled.

Sam looked back at Dev, checking out his chest.

Yes, I am a large, dear. Dev smiled sweetly.

A cotton T-shirt was tossed over a few heads. Sam caught it and passed it on to Dev.

Holding it out, Dev found a graphic of a "speed-racer" motorcycle rider on a red Kawasaki. In bold letters circling the rider was the words, "Leather Boys". "Couldn't get more phallic than that, guys."

Tony sneered, "We'll probably get the snot kicked out of us for being queer."

Dev darted his eyes to Tony. *Aha. First homophobe in the group. Well, it was bound to happen.*

"I love it." Sam admired the artwork.

"You have a hand in this, web-designer-man?" Dev teased.

"I did!" Sam replied proudly.

"Shoulda known." Tony shook his head.

"You don't have to wear it, Tony." Dev folded it up and set it on his lap so it wouldn't get dirty from the food plates.

"I'm not."

Dev touched Sam affectionately on his shoulder, whispering, "I love it."

"Thanks." Sam grinned happily back.

The older members and their significant others rose up in preparation for going home. Dev checked his watch, it was just before nine.

Tony folded his paperwork and picked up his helmet. "I'll see you guys Tuesday."

"See ya." Dev and Sam waved.

Wanting to invite Sam over on the pretext of talking about the trip, Dev was just about to ask when Sam scooted out his chair and gathered his things. "You have to get home?"

"I should. I have to get some work done tonight. Just some updates."

"Tonight?" Dev asked.

"Yeah. I promised I'd have them done by tomorrow and this meeting has put it back a few hours."

"Oh. Right." Dev felt disappointed.

"So? See you Tuesday?"

"You will." Dev wanted to touch him. He reached out for his hand. "It was great meeting you."

Smiling amiably, Sam grasped Dev's palm firmly. "Likewise."

With both of them now standing, Dev could see Sam's height matched his. Broad shoulders, narrow hips, long legs covered in soft blue denim, absolutely delicious.

Backing up, retrieving his helmet from the table, Dev watched Sam do the same. They paid their tab and walked out of the bar together. While Dev placed his helmet on his head and the T-shirt into his saddlebag, he admired Sam's bike and the way he appeared sitting on it. His tight, muscular thighs were straddling his cherry red Kawasaki and his powerful handling of it made Dev hard in his pants. Leaning it off its kickstand, Sam was gone in a flash of rumbling noise as Dev was left staring after with his mouth watering. Coming around from his fantasy, Dev sat on his bike, imagining he and Sam in the same tent on that flat plateau campsite in Sturgis.

"If this tent's rockin' don't come knockin'!" Dev muttered, wishful thinking. Waiting as more of their little club disbanded and vanished down the roadway, Dev left the parking lot headed to his condo, wanting Tuesday to arrive, and fast.

~

Coming through his doorway, taking off his jacket, and setting his helmet on the floor near the bedroom, Dev tossed the

T-shirt on his bed and sat at his computer, booting it up. As he waited for the screen to finish downloading, he typed in, "Sam Rhodes web designer".

The top of the list on Google was Sam's private domain name. Choking in shock at the title, Dev almost fell off his chair. *UNIX & MASTERS Web Designs by Rhodes*. The double-entendre was almost too obvious to believe. Dev clicked on every page to see if he could be proven wrong or right. The list of sites Sam hosted was long and impressive. One caught his interest. It was a gay advocate website. "Could it be?" Dev was beginning to think he was hoping for it so much, that he'd make up anything.

After digging as far as he could on the net for info, Dev shut the computer down and sat to think about it. "Well, Christ, it won't hurt to try."

Chapter Two

Dev spent the weekend before leaving for Sturgis finishing up on some edits he needed to complete on his latest novel. The next book he was writing was going to take place at the bike rally, so he considered it a business trip. Why not?

Packing a small kit with his camping gear, he included a digital camera. He wanted to take his laptop, but knew that was a luxury he didn't have space for, and with his luck it would be stolen. So, writing was put on hold for a week. Dev made sure his tent was in decent shape and attached an extra storage bag to his bike. His Kawasaki already had two hard saddlebags, but he decided on taking everything he could imagine needing. When his cell phone rang, Dev read the display and answered. "Hey, Dad."

"You excited?"

"Yeah, getting there."

"I wish I was coming with you."

Dev felt guilty.

As if sensing it, Jan said, "I'm just kidding. I'm too old to have fun there any longer."

"You know that's crap. There are guys in my club nearing sixty. I wish you'd let me hook you up with a side-car."

"Screw that!"

"Why? You used to take me there in one."

"You were a teen! Devlin, forget it. I had plenty of years there. It's your turn."

"You know Mom would love to go too."

"Not really. I asked her. She said she's had enough of the chaos."

"Huh." Dev looked down at his tent pensively as it lay on the concrete floor of the garage.

"So? How's the club?"

"It's a mixed bag."

"Anyone cute?"

Blushing instantly, Dev replied, "Shut up," laughing.

"Then there is!" his father teased.

"One guy."

"Is he gay?"

"I'm not sure."

"You gay men need to develop a secret handshake. I'm telling you it sucks not knowing."

"You're telling me? I've been punched in the face too many times."

"What's his name?"

"Sam. He's a web-designer. Get this, his company name is UNIX and Masters."

"He's gay."

"That would be my guess. But, hey, ya still gotta go slowly just in case."

"What are the other members like?"

"Older men. But I don't mind, Dad. They're more organized than the young ones. Jerry Macy has done a pretty decent job."

"Good."

"He's managed to get us T-shirts with the logo on it, and get this, in big letters it reads, 'Leather Boys.' Am I in for a thumping at Sturgis or what?"

"You better be careful, Dev. I mean it."

"It's bad enough I'm on a damn Kawasaki."

"No. I'm telling ya, they don't care anymore about the make of the bikes. They may tease you, but they won't start a fight over it. But…being gay? Please. Just don't kiss a man in public."

Dev felt slightly heartsick at that thought.

"Devlin."

"Yeah."

"I'm dead serious."

"I know, Dad."

"Don't make me come there and keep an eye on you."

"I wish you were." Dev laughed.

"Just be discreet. You can manage to keep your hands off this web-guy, what's his name?"

"Sam."

"Sam. Keep your paws off Sam until you get home. Promise me."

"I don't want to promise you that."

"Devlin!"

"Dad! If he's gay and we get drunk and we're in a tent together? Give me a break!"

"You don't get it."

"No," Dev replied, "I do get it. And I'll tell you another thing. I bet there are gay motorcycle groups going to Sturgis nowadays."

"No fucking way. It hasn't changed to that extent. And if they do go, they won't be waving the rainbow flag. Devlin, there are still plenty of good ol' boys riding to that place and they'd like nothing more than to beat a faggot to a pulp for kicks."

Dev shivered involuntarily.

"You there?"

"Yes." Dev sighed. "Look, let me finish loading the bike. I have to leave early Tuesday morning."

"You're taking your mobile phone I assume?"

"Yes."

"Good. If things go to shit and you need help, call and your Mom and I will come up to get you."

"Dad. I'm thirty."

"I don't give a shit how old you are. You still make shitty decisions."

"Don't throw that in my face again!" Dev moaned.

"Well? You married her!"

"Please. You have any idea how many times you remind me of my failed marriage?"

"You were gay in high school, Devlin!"

"All right, cut it out. I've heard it enough to last me a lifetime."

"Fine. I'll leave it for now. Wear your helmet and leathers to ride no matter how fucking hot you are. You got that?"

"Yes, Dad." Dev rolled his eyes.

"Don't patronize me, Devlin."

"Sorry. It's just that you know I will."

"Call me when you get there."

"I will. Is Mom around?"

"No. She went food shopping."

"All right. Tell her I'll talk to her soon."

"Be careful, son."

"I will, Dad." Dev hung up and stared at the phone as it shut down. Dropping it into his pocket, he went back to securing his camping equipment to his bike, brooding at having to hide his sexuality. He thought he'd left that horrible closet behind years ago.

~

After closing the garage and heading inside his condo, Dev heard his landline telephone ringing. Rushing to grab it, he picked it up and breathlessly said, "Hello?"

"Oh. Did I catch you at a bad time?"

"Sam?"

"Yes."

"No. It's a good time." Dev felt his skin tingle with warmth at the sound of Sam's voice. "I was just getting all my camping gear secured on the bike."

"I did the same. Look, since you've been there before, tell me what to bring."

Sitting down on his sofa with a view out of the sliding doors of his deck, Dev imagined Sam naked. "Well, to be honest, since the storage space on the bike is so limited, I bring only a change of underwear and a couple of T-shirts. It'll be hot in the day and cool at night. But don't get too bogged down with clothes."

"I had a feeling. So, like one pair of jeans, one pair of shorts?"

"Pretty much." Silence followed. Dev was dying to ask him over. "Anything else?"

"Are you bringing a sleeping bag?"

"Yes. Just that and a tent. I don't have the luxury of pillows or anything."

"I've got an inflatable."

"Oh, good thinking." Dev wished he could share it with him after a hot fuck.

"What about a first aid kit?"

"To be honest, they have excellent staff there if you get hurt, but I do bring a small kit for scratches or bug bites. I've got that covered if you're hurting for room."

"I'm so glad you're going with me."

Dev's cock perked up as his wishful thinking kicked in again. "Really?"

"Well, you've been there. I'm intimidated, Dev. I hate to admit it, but this event is so damn big."

"It is. It's huge and it's insane. Expect the unexpected."

"Like what?"

"The usual. Drunk parties, girls and guys flashing body parts, you know."

"Any fights?"

"Yeah. Some. You can tell the trouble-makers a mile away. Just hang with the normal looking people and not the trailer-park types."

"You know, when I first joined the club, I assumed we'd all be together. I'm surprised it's already turned into separate groups."

"I'm not. It happens that way. Especially when you're new." Dev really wanted to ask him over. But it was getting late and he was already tired. "It'll still be exciting to ride there as a group."

"True."

A long pause followed where they were just listening to each other breathe. Ironically, it didn't feel awkward to Dev. It felt natural. How weird was that?

"Am I keeping you?"

"No. I was just relaxing. Uh, what are you doing?" *Phone sex? Please? Tell me you're on your bed naked.*

"Trying to narrow down the essentials."

"You and I have the same bike. I noticed after the meeting when you took off."

"Really? That's cool."

"Do you just have the two saddlebags?"

"Yes. Why?"

"I got the extra one for the back of the seat. But I still have to strap the tent and sleeping back down."

"I know. There's no way to pack those in the sides."

It got quiet again.

"Mine's black."

"Huh?" Sam asked.

"My bike is black. I noticed yours was red."

"Oh. Right. I noticed your leather jacket was black as well."

Dev sat up on the couch, rubbing his hard cock as the excitement in him grew. Talking about their leathers? *Oh yes!* "Black, yes. I'll be cooking in them."

"You probably noticed mine. Red, white, and black. And yes, we'll cook. But it's better than leaving your flesh scraped off on the highway."

"No shit! I don't know how anyone can ride with a T-shirt, shorts, and no helmet."

"Me neither. Screw that." Sam laughed nervously. "I knew a guy who did that. Christ, the scars it left on his leg are fricken horrible. It ground him down to bone."

Dev shivered. His father had told him about accidents like that on more than one occasion. "I suggest we don't gross each other out with motorcycle accident horror stories."

"No. Good idea. I already know too many. My mom hates that I ride."

"Most do. I'm lucky in a way that my mom and dad used to ride all the time."

"Is your dad coming?"

"I wish he was. No. He was injured on the job. His riding days are over."

"Wow. Bad?"

"Bad enough. He was in construction and a steel beam fell on him. He's got metal plates in his leg and can't really get into a seated position for too long without being in agony."

"That sucks."

"Hell, at least he's alive."

At the next long pause, Sam said, "Well, I should let you go. See you at the Cracker Barrel in the morning."

"Yeah, uh, where did you say you were coming from?"

"Centerville."

"I live in Centerville. Where in Centerville do you live?" Dev's heart raced faster.

"Right off of East Whipp."

"No shit? Where?"

"A little condo complex on Berrycreek."

"Shit! I live close by you. I'm right off Bigger Road."

"Really?"

"Yeah."

"That's great. You want to meet here and we'll go to the Cracker Barrel together?"

"Yes!" Dev couldn't wait to see him.

"Let me give you my address."

Dev hopped off the couch and scrambled for a pen and paper. "Shoot." He wrote it down and felt his heart beating like crazy. "Okay. I'll be there about quarter of?"

"Cool!"

"Then..." Dev didn't want to hang up. "Then, I'll see you in the morning."

"Try to get some sleep. We have a long ass-killing ride tomorrow."

Tempted to say he'd massage Sam's sore ass, Dev bit his tongue. "Yes. I will. See ya."

"See ya."

He hung up and stared at his address. "Christ, Sam, you are almost walking distance from here." Pumping his fist in the air, Dev only needed one thing. For Sam to be gay.

Chapter Three

Even though he set his alarm for six, he was up before it. Hopping out of bed, showering and shaving quickly, Dev dressed in his black leather slacks and jacket knowing he was going to boil. Making a last check that everything was secure in his condo, and he had all that he needed to bring with him, he locked the door and jogged down the stairs to the detached garage. Using his remote, he elevated the door and found his iron horse waiting like a proud steed. Jiggling all the camping gear to make sure it was secure, he prepped the engine and turned the key. After adjusting the choke, he clipped his helmet strap under his jaw and flipped down the visor.

The morning air was still cool and refreshing as he rode. Five minutes later he pulled into another condo complex. As he slowed to read the numbers on the buildings, he found a leather-clad man waving him down. Seeing Sam dressed that way made his cock instantly respond. Pulling next to Sam's bike in the garage, Dev shut off his engine and flipped up his face shield. "Good morning!"

"Good morning!" Sam smiled, his brown eyes shining. "I am so pumped for this!"

Dev hiked his bike up on its kickstand and climbed off. Taking a minute to devour the sight of this hunk from his mane of brown hair to his leather boots, Dev wished they were already a couple and he could grab him where he wanted to grab him. Namely, his tight ass and bulging crotch.

"Wow, look at you!" Sam shook his head in admiration. "Sexy black leather rider."

That comment reeked of a come-on in Dev's book. "You like?" Dev spun around for him so Sam could admire his backside as well.

"Nice!" Looking down at his own outfit, Sam asked, "Do I look like a dork?"

Choking at the totally inaccurate appraisal, Dev had to hold back so he wouldn't drool down his chinstrap. "Uh. No. You look like anything but a dork."

"Really?"

At the seductive gaze he was receiving, Dev opened his mouth to ask flat out, Are you gay? But before he got the chance, Sam said, "We'd better go," and busily checked that things were secure on his bike, placing his helmet on his head.

"Right." Dev straddled his seat and started his engine.

Walking the five hundred pound-plus machine backwards to give Sam room to turn around in the garage, Dev waited. Sam closed the garage door, and nodded he was ready. As Sam accelerated out of the parking area, Dev was in heat staring at him. The man was so fucking gorgeous, and in that leather riding outfit, on that cherry red crotch-rocket, Dev knew his briefs were already damp with pre-come just from looking at the guy. *Christ, what a cock-tease you are, Rhodes!*

Keeping up with him down Bigger Road to Clyo and flying up Wilmington Pike, Dev kept imagining their first kiss. Alone, in a tent, in the dark. *God, hold me back I'm going to die.*

Since they were so close by, they were pulling into the graded curved lot in a matter of minutes. Ten bikes were already parked in a neat row as the members loitered and talked together, waiting for everyone to arrive.

Dev's excitement at the coming ride and event was making him giddy. Pulling up next to Sam, closing the engines down in sync, Dev took off his helmet and smiled brightly at him. "I'm going to love this."

"Me too." Sam grinned, as if he was already high. "Look. There's macho-Tony."

Oh, you are so gay! Dev made the decision. He had to be. "Yeah. Let's go say hi."

Strutting side by side in their snazzy leather uniforms, Dev felt like a member of the *A-Team*, or *CSI*, or *Miami Vice*, or something.

"Mr. Spagna," Sam greeted him. "You're looking fine in your hot Harley outfit."

Dev thought that was a very bold way to address a blatantly heterosexual man, but it seemed Sam was so damn attractive he could get away with it.

"I am, if I say so myself!" Tony smoothed his hand down his broad leather chest.

Taking a closer look at him, Dev asked, "You get punched in the eye, Tony?"

A look of frustration washed the pride away from Tony's face.

Sam held Tony's arm in concern. "What the hell happened?"

"Nothin'. Fergetaboutit," He said in a heavy New York accent. "I'm starved. Who are we waiting for?"

Sam shouted, "Jerry? Who's left?"

"Just Ralph and Douglas!"

"Why don't we grab some seats? They'll have to push some tables together for a mob this big."

"Go on, Sam. June and I will wait."

Nodding, Sam headed into the restaurant which was set up so you had to pass through their gift shop first.

Eying the collection of strange ceramics and knickknacks, Dev made sure he didn't knock anything over as they met the hostess.

"How many?"

Sam looked back at Dev with a pained expression.

"Tell her fifteen," Dev offered. "I don't think we're that many but just in case."

She heard and asked them to wait. As they did, Tony picked up a DVD from a display and shouted, "Hey, look! They have old television shows on DVD for sale. Check this out. *Welcome Back Kotter*," he laughed, sticking it back into the rack.

"Yeah, and you're Vinnie Barbarino," Sam yelled.

Leaning towards Sam, Dev whispered, "Bet his wife did that."

"No. Punched him in the eye? Come on."

"Bet ya." Dev leaned against Sam as he stared at Tony.

"Poor guy."

"Yeah, no kidding." Not wanting to stop touching him, Dev had no choice when the hostess waved that she was ready. A line of leather-clad bikers descended on the restaurant dining area. Luckily it was early enough that not too many other patrons were present. Chairs rustled on the wood flooring, helmets settled under the table, and menus were handed around. Dev sat next to Sam, he'd have it no other way, and across from the black-eyed Tony Spagna.

"They have the best pancakes here." Sam licked his lips.

"Sold." Dev set his menu down.

When Sam smiled at him, Dev winked. *Big deal, so I like him, so sue me*. It seemed to agree with Sam because he blushed crimson.

With that hunk in leather sitting right next to him, Dev had to sit on his hands not to grope the man's leg. But he was sure now he was getting the right vibes. The. Vibes. The ones that said, "Go on, I'm interested."

"What will you have, Tony?" Sam placed his menu on top of Dev's on the table.

"I don't know. You guys are both getting pancakes? What are ya now, twins?"

Dev just laughed and Sam didn't answer.

"Nah. I want the eggs, sausage, you know. Man food." Tony teased.

"You're too manly for us, Tony."

When Sam said that, Dev choked in amazement. Looking up at Tony, it seemed it didn't have the same effect on him. Tony just smiled wryly. "I'm too manly for most people. Get used to it."

The waitress took their order efficiently and poured coffee for all. Opening the small plastic containers of cream, Dev dumped a few into his cup, observing Sam liked his the same way. Yet another thing in common. Dev was already imagining them domesticated and fixing breakfast together.

"You said you were a writer?" Tony asked, sipping his cup of black coffee.

"Yes."

"Do you write under your real name?"

"Yes, I do."

"How come I've never heard of you?" Tony kept his coffee near his mouth.

"I'm not exactly well known."

"Did you actually publish anything?"

Dev noticed Sam hanging on every word. "I have."

"What are they called? Tell me some titles. Maybe I'll recognize them."

Knowing unless the macho Italian stud Tony Spagna read erotic gay fiction, he doubted it very much. "You won't know them."

"How the fuck do you know?" Tony challenged. "I'm a big reader. I'm not some dumb shit."

"I know you're not a dumb shit. You teach, for Christ's sake." Dev wished they would change the subject.

"Well? Give me a title."

Looking over at Sam who was staring at his face intently, Dev sighed, "Fine. *Flying High*."

"*Flying High*? What the hell's it about? The air force?"

"No. Never mind. So, Sam..." Dev smiled sweetly at him. "I found your website for your business on the net. Interesting name."

"Yeah?" Sam grinned wickedly.

"What's the name?" Tony asked as the waitress went around the table refilling their cups.

Doug and Ralph had finally joined them with Jerry and June completing the group.

"It's UNIX and Masters."

"Eunuchs?" Tony curled his nose in repugnance. "Like in men without balls?"

Dev covered his laughter as Sam didn't and broke up with it. "No, Tony, as in the computer program. U-N-I-X."

"Sounds like some sick joke about men singing soprano." Tony shook his head.

"And you sound like one of the Sopranos," Dev teased.

"Hey, not all Italians are in the mob. So quit the stereotyping, Dev."

"I'm joking." Dev thanked the waitress as his cup was topped up. "No offense, Tony."

"None taken."

Their plates began arriving.

"Christ, look at the size of those pancakes," Tony gasped.

"See. Man food!" Dev grinned.

"Shit. I hope my plate is that full." He leaned up to look at the next round of dishes arriving at the table.

Sam announced, "If you want one, I'll give you one of mine."

"No. Thanks, Sam. I think this will do me." Tony began devouring his meal.

Leaning on Sam's shoulder, Dev whispered, "You're such a sweetie."

"Am I?" Sam's eyes gleamed as he replied.

On the tip of Dev's tongue was, "Oh, you are too gorgeous," but he couldn't say it for so many reasons. "Yes. You are."

"Thanks, Dev."

"My pleasure."

As they ate their meal, knowing it would have to hold them for several hours, Jerry started giving instructions.

"If any of you get tired or need a bathroom break, come up to the front with me and June and let us know and we'll take the next rest stop exit. If we get separated, we'll pull off again at the next highway rest area. I don't want to actually leave the highway and get off track, so stick to the highway rest stops. Oh, and by the way, Interstate 75 is crap in the beginning. The road surface is a mess. A trooper friend of Doug's told him to use caution because it's a real rough ride from the bad winter we just had and all the salt. No potholes, but plenty of pits and ridges. It's going to be a real nightmare until we get to 90."

Dev could already imagine how sore he was going to feel.

"If anyone has any trouble, again, make sure we're all aware, whatever it is. We stop as a group. Let's at least get there as one unit. We'll do the best we can after that. We can always meet up for an event or dinner. Speaking of that, here are all our mobile phone numbers."

A pile of paper was passed around.

"You all have your T-shirts with you?"

Everyone yelled "yeah" except Tony who kept eating.

"Good. Alright. Let's finish up, take our last pit-stop, and get going."

"Where's your shirt, Tony?" Dev asked impishly.

"You think I'm going to get the shit kicked out of me for wearing a gay shirt?"

"Gay?" Sam appeared insulted.

"Looks like someone already beat the shit out of you," Dev whispered.

"Shut the fuck up."

Dev held up his hands in defense. "I've got to make a pit-stop. Too much coffee."

"Me too." Sam stood up with Dev, both taking their helmets with them.

Standing next to Sam at a urinal, Dev couldn't resist a peek. *Oh, yes. Very nice!* "So, uh, that Tony, he's a real piece of work."

"Just the usual macho man. Don't let him get to you." Sam gave his dick a shake and turned to face Dev.

When he did, full on, Dev almost died at the sight and the obvious invitation to take a look at what Sam was packing under his thick cowhide slacks. From that point on, Dev was convinced he and Sam were of the same ilk. Watching Sam tuck his fantastic dick away in his leathers, Dev had to beat his back before it grew hard. Though Dev wanted to compliment Sam on his hot anatomy, Dev found too many of their club members gathered around.

They stood at the sink together washing their hands. Dev replied, "He doesn't get to me. I just feel sorry for the guy. I wouldn't want to have to prove I'm manly on a daily basis."

"Christ no!" Sam laughed, handing Dev paper towels.

"Thanks." Dev dried his hands and dumped the paper in the trash as they exited the room. Holding his helmet under his arm, Dev stood in the long line to pay their individual tabs. Once they had and regrouped in the parking lot, Jerry was there to shout more instructions.

"Get on 675 northbound to 75! Got it?"

Dev waved, clipping the chinstrap of his helmet. Making sure Sam was ready, Dev waited as he started his bike and parked next to Sam in the winding string of motorcycles.

The sun shining and warm, they moved as one long serpentine line to the entrance ramp and merged onto the highway. Once Jerry got them at cruising speed, around seventy to seventy-five miles per hour, Dev began to get excited again. Looking over at Sam who was riding beside him in the lane, he noticed the rest rode mostly in single file or two by two, in an unbroken train and looking very cool. Dev wished he could film it.

Here we go! An adventure of lifetime. Five hundred thousand bikers all in one place. Amazing.

Before they had even ridden ten miles, Tony seemed to be frustrated with the pace and passed them all in the speed lane. Dev looked over at Sam who shook his head in reply. Straining to check over the group, for he and Sam were about mid-way, Dev could see Tony riding along side Jerry and his wife, June, who was on the back seat of his Jerry's Harley.

Dev could imagine Tony shouting at Jerry to speed up, but seventy-five in a sixty-five mile per hour zone was fast enough. They passed so many state highway patrol cars, no one wanted the ticket. Yes, the cops knew it was the Sturgis week and yes, they even had an ex-state trooper with them, but why push their luck? And the damn highway surface was brutal. It was bad enough at that speed trying to keep from getting sucked into a rut or bouncing over patched cracks and potholes. Dev wished he could shout something at Sam, but the noise was way too loud. And the bugs smashing his helmet windscreen were gross and distracting.

Their first break came in Toledo, right on the Michigan border and before they hit I90.

Dev's ass was already aching, not to mention his back. He wondered how the older men were holding up.

Pulling off in a nice neat line in front of two buildings, one with toilets, one with vending machines, Dev shut the bike and sat up, groaning at the stiffness in his joints.

The minute they stopped moving, the heat hit. Taking off his helmet, Dev rubbed his face and hair in exhaustion.

"Christ, I'm beat," Sam moaned.

Turning to look at him, Dev found his weariness reflected in Sam.

"Look at this." Sam showed Dev his helmet indicating the bugs. "Gross!"

"I know. But imagine them hitting your face."

Using his leather sleeve, Sam tried to wipe them off.

"Come on. Let's go take a piss." Dev managed to get his leg over his bike and stand. "Christ, my ass is vibrating."

"Ooh, baby!" Sam laughed.

Dev smiled wickedly. "Not in a good way."

Turning away shyly, Sam led the way to the men's room. As he followed, Dev drooled over his bottom and legs in tight leather. *You hot mother-fucker! Flirting with me like that! You are so going to get it!* Dev set his helmet down and waited his turn at the urinals. He and Sam once again were side by side. Dev wondered if he would get another good look at that lovely dick of his.

"Damn, I had to go ages ago." Sam whimpered as he let loose his stream.

"Me too. That's the fucking coffee."

"Christ, remind me no coffee before long hauls."

Dev peeked over at Sam's crotch. *Well? Let's see it.* Pausing, giving his a shake, Dev wondered if Sam was going to grant him another grand frontal view. As if he were thinking about it, Sam took a look around the area. Their group of men practically surrounded them. The little show was put on hold. Dev certainly understood why.

He followed Sam to the sinks to wash their hands and helmets. Using soft soap, Dev scrubbed the insect goo off the face shield.

"Yech. That is so sick." Sam winced.

"You know, some of those hardcore Harley riders don't even wear a helmet. Just sunglasses. They pick this shit out of their teeth."

"Did your dad wear a helmet?"

Smiling shyly, Dev replied, "Mom made him."

"I don't blame her."

They wiped their helmets dry and left the building. Tony was leaning on his hog eating a candy bar.

"Want something?" Dev pointed to the vending machines.

"Sure."

Dev took out a crisp dollar bill. "Which one?"

"Uh, how about a Kit Kat?"

"My favorite." Dev pushed the buttons for two. They fell down off the coil and change jingled into the dish.

"Here." Sam tried to hand Dev money.

"My treat." Dev pocketed his own coins and gave Sam one of the chocolate bars.

"You want to hang out with Tony?"

"Why not." Dev held the door open and they met up with the handsome Italian man.

"Did you tell Jerry to go faster?" Sam asked, breaking off one of the rows of his Kit Kat bar.

"Yeah. Christ, at this pace we'll never get there."

Chewing his treat, Dev replied, "The road surface sucks. Seventy-five is fast enough. Besides, you see all the damn troopers?"

"I just want to get there."

"Us too." Dev finished his chocolate bar.

"Geez, do you two do everything alike?" Tony pointed to the Kit Kats. "Better watch it or people will get the wrong idea."

Dev puffed up in defense. "What's that supposed to mean?"

Sam grabbed Dev's arm, dragging him back. "Ignore him."

"Maybe that's why you got a sock in the eye, Tony. Your big fucking mouth!"

"Dev," Sam implored. "It's not worth it."

"No, Dev," Tony sneered, "I got a sock in the eye because my wife thinks I'll cheat on her with another woman, not a man."

Dev grabbed Tony's jacket and snarled into his smug expression. Sam intervened and pushed Dev back.

"I thought I liked you, asshole," Dev shouted at Tony. "But I changed my fucking mind!"

35

"Think I give a shit?" Tony laughed.

"Nice to know a fucking homophobe is teaching children!"

"Dev," Sam chided, leading them back to where they parked their bikes.

With Sam nudging him back to their Kawasakis, Dev muttered in fury, "Goddamn asshole…"

"Calm down." Sam laughed. "If you think that's bad, what are you going to do at Sturgis?"

Facing Sam, Dev met his trusting eyes. "I hate schmucks like that, Sam. I just think everyone has the right to decide. You know?"

"Yes. I do. So don't let him get to you, okay?"

Jerry shouted loudly. "Let's go! I90 West! Through Chicago, people! Follow signs for Madison, Wisconsin."

Dev put his helmet on, but his mood did not improve. He and Sam hadn't even done anything and already he was being accused. Great.

Back on his bike, his ass and back aching, Dev couldn't wipe the snarl off his face…until Sam smiled sweetly and gave him a thumb's up. Instantly his heart melted.

~

It was becoming torture. Dev didn't know how much more he could take. He was exhausted, starving, and once again had to piss. About to take the left lane to flag Jerry down and insist on a break, the minute they made it to Sioux Falls, Jerry led the caravan off the interstate. They ended up at a KOA only a few minutes from the highway. Dev was so glad to rest his ass he could cry.

Finally stopped, Dev flipped up his face shield. "See? We may have had some doubts about the older guys in the group, but here we are at a KOA in Sioux Falls. Not bad for bunch of old farts."

"They did great. Christ, I can't wait to get off this bike. I never thought I say that. But, I'm dyin'." Sam stretched his back.

Jerry waved after checking them all in. The line of motorcycles moved slowly in a double column to a nice grassy area with trees for shade near a building Dev hoped was toilets and showers.

Parking, getting off his bike, Dev removed his helmet and stretched his back in agony. "Oh, man! I am beat!"

"These Kawasakis aren't really made for long hauling." Sam moaned setting his helmet on the seat and taking off his leather jacket.

Seeing his logo on his shirt, Dev smiled. "All of us in the same T-shirt. We'll look like such dorks."

Sam shrugged. Pointing he said, "That's a good spot for a tent."

"It is." Dev checked out the shady soft grass.

"After a piss we should set them up."

"Good idea." Dev put his helmet down and shook out his legs as he walked. "Christ, I'm numb."

Entering the cool interior, relieving himself and washing his face, Dev checked out his reflection. His light brown hair was flat from being sweaty and under a helmet and he couldn't wait to shower.

Seeing Sam watching him, Dev smiled shyly. "I feel like I look like crap."

"I hear ya." Sam splashed his face.

"Right. Tent." Dev tried to motivate them. "I'm starved. I don't think there's a restaurant here."

"We passed one on the way in."

Dev moaned, "Back on the bike? Torture!"

When Sam smiled and patted his back, Dev twisted around to catch his eye. But he didn't. Sam's gaze was back on their motorcycles.

Tossing his jacket over his bike seat, Dev untied his tent and went about setting it up. Soon tiny pup tents were erected, two side by side. Opening the front zipper, Dev tossed his jacket and sleeping bag inside it, then dug around his saddlebag for his shorts. After finding them, he said to Sam, "I need a shower desperately."

"Me too. I was just going to check with Jerry to see what everyone was doing for dinner."

Following Sam, noticing that Tony had set up next to Ralph and avoided eye contact with them, Dev paused as Sam approached Jerry and June.

"You guys heading back out for dinner later?"

"Oh, no! We're stoking up a nice barbeque. We've got all the fixings. Just bring yourself along."

"What about booze?" Dev asked.

"Couldn't carry all that, son. But there is a store close by."

"Screw it." Dev was too tired.

"Thanks, Jerry. It was nice of you to bring all the food." Sam smiled sweetly.

"My pleasure. We'll be at Sturgis tomorrow, so this may be our last get together as a whole club before everyone gets lost."

"True!" Sam nodded, waving as he walked back to where Dev was standing.

"Damn. I'd love a beer." Dev headed to their tents with Sam.

"I'll go."

"No. I can't ask you to do that."

"I don't mind."

"Look. Hop on the back of mine. I'll take us together."

"Good idea."

Though he was fatigued and dying to lie down, Dev put his jacket and helmet on. Straddling the bike, he waited for Sam to climb on the back.

Once they were on their way out of the campsite, Dev realized how nice it felt to have Sam with him, resting against him. Very nice indeed!

Losing his concentration from being overtired and sore, Dev felt the press of Sam's body behind him from his hips to his lower back. He imagined Sam was holding the back of the bike because his arms weren't visible when Dev tried to look. He desperately wanted Sam to wrap around him, hugging him tight from behind, and wondered if that's what Sam wanted as well, but it was just too early to attempt that kind of contact.

About to shout out to Sam that he should hold onto his waist, Dev didn't get the chance when Sam pointed out a small grocery store only a few yards from the front of the campsite's main entrance. Parked, Dev waited for Sam to climb off before he set the bike up on its stand and entered the tiny shop.

He was so hungry, he felt as if he could load up on junk food. Following Sam to the beer cooler, they stood to assess the quality of the selection.

"Crap. It sucks." Dev leaned against Sam's shoulder. Something he felt very comfortable doing.

"I know. Looks like piss beer or nothing."

"How about this one?" Dev picked up a six pack.

"All those mass produced beers taste the same to me."

"Should we get chips or pretzels?"

"Pretzels…and bottled water."

"Good thinking."

They set their items up on the counter.

"You boys headin' to Sturgis?"

"We are." Dev smiled and took out some cash.

"I thought so. Every moto-cycle rider in the country goes." He was missing a tooth. "That'll be thirteen dollars and fifteen cents, please."

"I bet even though you're miles from it, you'll get full up." Sam took the bag of items.

"Oh, we do all right."

"Thanks." Dev waved to him, asking Sam, "You want me to try and stick that in the saddlebags?"

"I've got it." Sam handed it off temporarily as he put on his helmet.

Dev mounted the bike and waited for Sam to get on. He gave Sam back the shopping bag before he started the engine up. Driving more slowly with Sam's hands full, Dev returned to their tents and, this time, definitely did not want to ride again for a few hours. Waiting for Sam to dismount before he set the bike up on the kickstand, Dev felt the tight brush of Sam's body against his own and closed his eyes to savor it.

Taking off his helmet and jacket, Dev watched Sam for a moment just to admire his incredible physique.

While Dev stood still, the sweat began to drip down his face. His thoughts back on the notion of a shower, he found a small kit with his toiletries and said, "I'll be back before that beer gets warm."

After he hid the food in his tent, Sam said, "Wait. I'll join you."

Join me in a shower? Could I get that lucky? Dev watched as Sam hurried to catch up. Once Sam had what he needed, he gestured for Dev to go. As they walked together, Dev deliberately brushed Sam's arm, wanting to touch him, dying for contact.

To his dismay Dev found several others from their group had the same idea.

No nookie for now, I'm afraid. But Dev did wonder after a few beers and darkness if he could make a pass.

Finally taking off his shirt and hot leather pants, Dev stood under a showerhead and didn't wait for it to warm up. He was so overheated he enjoyed the cold spray. Thinking of Sam naked and wet, Dev felt his cock bob in excitement and entertained the idea of a quick release. Deciding to stay horny and go on the hunt for satisfaction with Sam later, Dev scrubbed clean, allowing his hormones to surge in expectation.

Shutting off the taps, he sighed happily and wiped his face with a towel. When he opened the shower curtain he caught sight of Sam naked from behind, drying off. "Holy shit..." Dev paused, covering his instant hard-on with his towel. *You fantastic fucker!* Licking his lips as he drooled, Dev imagined a very passionate night. Noticing other men he knew from their group coming and going, he found Tony staring directly at him. Dev frowned in reflex and moved out of the stall to where he had left his things. Slipping on his shorts, sans briefs, Dev got busy brushing his hair in the mirror, trying to get his body to soften up and behave.

"Hey."

As Sam stood next to him, his shaggy brown hair longer when wet, brushing his shoulders and covering his ears, Dev's body misbehaved once again.

"You ready for that beer? Lukewarm or otherwise?"

"We should have bought ice." Forcing his gaze away from Sam's slender body, Dev packed his things back in his kit.

"We should have brought a camper van with a fridge and beds, but you have to draw the line somewhere."

Following Sam out, ogling his tight ass in his tiny blue gym shorts, lacking underwear lines, *oh, my God*, and shirtless with that tiny dragon tattoo exposed, Dev knew he couldn't control

41

his dick under these circumstances no matter how hard he tried. Still using his damp towel as a crotch shield, Dev made it back to their little cozy site and tucked his things away in the hard saddlebag of his bike, tossing his wet towel over his tent to dry. Sitting down on the grass, retrieving the beer from Sam's outstretched hand, Dev took a quick peek at his own body to check how obvious his hard dick was. Very. He only hoped Sam didn't look. Or if he looked, he wanted it hard.

Sitting nearby on the shady grass, Sam sighed tiredly after his first sip of cheap beer. "I am so glad to be off that bike. I swear I was in pain."

"I know. It's not the best bike for touring."

"That's an understatement."

Dev couldn't stop staring at him. Sam was so damn beautiful. He had angular contours under his high cheekbones, hollows that made his face rugged and masculine. His nose was narrow at the bridge and flared slightly at the tip, and his lips were full and soft looking. Those rich, dark, chocolate eyes were hypnotic.

The smooth tanned skin of Sam's chest, his cut abs, almost hairless torso except for a soft patch in an inverted triangle between his pectoral muscles, was turning Dev on so much, he was beginning to feel like he had the devil and angel on his shoulders arguing on jumping this man's bones.

"I smell barbeque. You think Jerry will call us for some grub?" Sam sniffed the air.

"He'd better." Dev leant up. "I can see them from here. Jerry's flipping food on a grill."

When Sam twisted around to look, Dev gave his crotch a good once over. He could be wrong, but a semi-hard large penis appeared to be lurking under those tight gym shorts.

"I'm starved. This lousy beer will go right to my head."

"Oh?" Dev smiled. "Are you a cheap drunk?"

"Yes. Don't tell." Sam winked.

It was so sexy, Dev was sure it was flirting. "Promise. Are you a horny drunk?"

"Would it terrify you if I am?"

Dev lit on fire. "It would scare me senseless." He went along with the game.

"I'll make sure I don't mistake you for a voluptuous woman."

"Believe me. You won't make that mistake."

Just as Dev anticipated a very seductive reply, Doug made his way over. "Jerry said to tell you the food is ready."

"Cool," Dev responded, but in reality he was cursing the interruption. "Uh, you think we should share the beer?"

"Four bottles?" Sam laughed. "That won't go very far."

"True." Dev drank his down, setting the empty near the tent. As he stood, he checked his crotch. Annoyed he was still partially erect, he pushed the heel of his palm on it trying to tame it, but it wasn't an easy task. When he looked up, Sam was watching.

Shit.

"You all right?" Sam asked, that impish twinkle to his eyes.

"Riding always gives me wood."

"Oh? Blaming it on the ride?"

"Aren't you?" Dev gestured to Sam's crotch.

Without a word, Sam grinned wickedly, spun around and strutted to the others.

Dev was in agony watching his ass, but had to calm down.

Smelling roasting meat, Dev finally diverted his leer away from Sam's perfect buttocks to see Tony glaring at him. About punch the sneer off his face, Dev felt Sam's hand on his arm. Meeting his eyes, Sam whispered, "Don't."

"How the fuck did you get to know me so well so soon?"

Sam just smiled in reply.

A line had formed and Jerry was using a tong to dole out the various meats he had barbequed. A table was set up with hamburger and hot dog rolls and ketchup.

A paper plate in his hand, Dev forced himself to drop the scowl he had on his face from Tony and thanked Jerry. "You're great. Thanks for doing this."

"Your dues has to pay for something!" Jerry laughed. "Burger or dog?"

"Dog."

Jerry put a hot dog on Dev's plate. He stood at the condiment table and stuck the hotdog into a bun, squeezing ketchup on the roll. Feeling someone brush his arm, he was about to get violent thinking it was Tony when he realized it was Sam.

"A wiener for you as well?" Sam laughed.

"Don't get naughty."

"It's hard not to."

"Behave." Dev was about to crack up when Tony appeared.

"You two in the same tent?"

"What the fuck do you care if we are?" Dev growled. "What the hell's it got to do with you?"

"Why didn't you join a fucking gay club? Why taint ours?"

"Taint?" Dev was about to deck him.

"Will you two cut it out?" Sam ordered. "Once we get to the rally believe me, we don't have to bump into each other."

"Yeah, but I'm at your damn campsite and you're both members of my club."

"Your club?" Dev snarled. "You mean Jerry Macy's club?"

"Does he know you're both queer?" Tony's nose curled in repugnance.

"How the hell did you come up with the idea we were gay?" Sam asked, exasperated.

"Gay-dar! Duh!' Tony mocked, eating his hamburger.

"That's really fucked up, Tony. Why don't you go eat with someone who doesn't think you're a complete idiot?" Sam turned his back to him.

When Tony walked away, Dev asked, "Are you upset he thinks we're gay? Or upset he thinks we're gay?"

"Do you realize you just asked me the same question twice?" Sam chewed his food.

"It only sounded like the same question." Dev bit into the hotdog.

Sam took a long while to think about it. "I have no idea how you want me to answer you."

"Fine. Never mind. You think we can get seconds?" Dev stuffed the remainder of his bun into his mouth.

"Go look."

Dev walked back to the line. As it dwindled he noticed so did the food. Giving up, he walked passed Tony and Ralph, who obviously was Tony's new co-conspirator, and returned to Sam. "There's really nothing left. I'm going back to the tent."

"I'll be there soon. I just want to ask Jerry about what we're doing in the morning."

After acknowledging him and leaving, Dev headed back to their two bikes. He took out his mobile phone that was inside his leather jacket pocket and sat down on the grass.

"Hey."

"You get there?" his father asked.

"No. We got as far as Sioux Falls. Everyone is beat."

"Well, you have time. No reason to push yourselves. How's your ass?"

"Sore!" Dev laughed. "Is Mom there?"

"Hang on...Melinda! Dev's on the phone!"

"Baby?"

"Hiya, Ma." Dev smiled at her voice.

45

"How's my cutie-pie?"

Jan said, "His ass is sore."

"So? Get a nice young man to massage it for you."

"I'm working on it." Dev looked for Sam.

"How's the bike holding out?" Jan asked.

"It's brand new, Dad. It better hold out."

"I'm just used to my old hogs. Had to keep putting oil in those damn things."

"Not my girl. No way." Dev laughed.

"Is the group okay, Devie?"

"It's not bad, Mom. There's one guy I like."

"Is he gay?"

"Christ, I hope so."

"Just find a nice doobie and smoke it with him."

"Ma, you're like something out of the Seventies."

"She *is* something out of the Seventies, Dev," Jan chuckled. "Don't smoke dope until you get there. I don't want you riding high."

"Dad, I don't smoke pot."

"Where did we get him, Jan?" Melinda asked.

"I have no idea, cookie," Jan replied.

"All right, cut it out. Let me go, Sam is coming."

"Is that his name?"

"Yes, Mom. I'll call you tomorrow."

"Good luck getting laid, cutie-pie!"

"Goodbye, Mom!" he choked in amazement. "Bye, Dad." He disconnected and tossed the phone back into his coat pocket.

Sam sat down next to him. "Jerry figures we can get up around eight or nine."

"Okay."

"Checking in with the girlfriend?" Sam gestured to Dev's jacket which was lying on the grass nearby.

"No. Look, Sam…"

"Want another beer?"

"Yes, please." Sam handed him a beer and the bag of pretzels. Dev twisted the top off the bottle, pulling open the pretzel bag and taking a few to gnaw on, frustrated with Tony and the mystery of Sam's preference. Reclining, drinking the beer, Dev looked out at the landscape in the distance.

"What mountain do you think that is?" Sam asked, lying beside him.

"I have no clue. It's not even really big enough to call a mountain."

"Christ, it feels good to lie flat." Sam dropped down to the grass. "My back is toast."

"I know. It's hard leaning over for that long."

"I swear I can feel shooting pains running down my lower back."

"You…" Dev swallowed the pretzel with the beer. "You want me to rub you a little? You know, just to ease the pain?"

"I'd love it. You kidding? But the grief we'd get from Tony, and who knows who else…"

"I can do it inside one of our tents when it gets darker."

"You sure you don't mind?"

"Yes. I mean no. I don't mind." Dev felt his dick hardening again at the idea of being able to get his hands on him.

"I'll return the favor."

"Good." Dev instantly imagined reciprocal blowjobs. He gulped more beer, begging for the sun to set. It seemed it never did in August.

"I don't get guys like him."

"Well, judging from the black eye, I assume his wife doesn't get him either."

Sam rolled to his side, propping his head up in his palm as he sipped his beer. "Yeah, about that. Why is she married to him if she doesn't trust him?"

"I bet he got her pregnant."

"No. He said he didn't have kids. Remember? He has enough noise from the kids in class."

"Maybe he persuaded her to terminate it."

"Then why marry her?"

"Who knows." Dev shrugged. "I am so fucking tired."

"Me too. Am I keeping you up?"

"No. Not really. I'm enjoying sitting here with you."

"I'm glad." Sam smiled at him as he consumed more beer. "So, you were married? Now divorced?"

"Christ, you have a good memory."

"I didn't remember everyone's story. Just a few."

"Oh?" Dev finished his beer and set the empty with the first one. He took his towel off the tent and curled it up like a pillow to rest his head on. "What do you want to know?"

"Well, how long were you married?"

"Seven years."

"Seven-year itch?"

"Maybe."

"Did you cheat?"

"No. Neither of us did."

"What happened?"

Dev didn't want to say. Not yet. Not before knowing for certain what Sam thought about alternative lifestyles.

"Am I getting too personal? Sorry."

"I suppose I am guarded. I don't know you, Sam."

"No. I suppose you don't. Not really. But I have to admit I feel like I've known you longer than a few days. We click."

"Do we?" Dev felt his cock twitch again.

"Don't you think? I mean, I'm looking forward to doing this thing with you."

Dev's heart went into overdrive. "Doing what thing?"

"Sturgis."

Slightly let down, Dev nodded. "Oh, right."

"What did you think I meant?"

"Never mind. Look, I'm going to brush my teeth and take a last piss before I crash. I'm exhausted."

"I'll join you."

They headed back to the bathroom. It was nearly vacant. Dev noticed a condom dispenser and wondered if he should buy one. Sam was leaning over a sink, brushing his teeth.

Dev took out some change and tried to be casual as he pushed coins into the dispenser. Once he pocketed the packet he found Sam staring.

"Going to get lucky?" Sam smiled.

His cheeks on fire with humiliation, Dev loaded his toothbrush. "You never know." Seeing Sam staring at his ass in the mirror's reflection, Dev rinsed his mouth and looked back at him. For a moment they gazed at each other. Dev wished he knew what Sam was thinking. Making a deliberate sweep down Sam's body, there, under those tight blue shorts was an enormous erection.

The noise of men's voices entering the toilet broke their trance. Dev followed Sam out of the room quickly. Stuffing his toiletries back into the saddlebag, Dev asked, "Your tent or mine?"

Sam looked back at the group of club members sitting and relaxing at picnic tables. It wasn't dark yet. Just turning dusk.

"Do you care?" Dev asked.

"Unfortunately I do."

Finding the spot they had laid on previously, Dev reclined once more, again using his towel as a pillow and staring up at the tree they were under, which moved slightly in a balmy breeze.

"Don't you think it's already bad enough with Tony's teasing?"

Dev looked over at Sam who was resting next to him. "I don't give a shit about that asshole."

"No? Not even if he makes our life miserable for six days?"

"How's he going to do that?"

"Can you imagine him pointing us out to some fucking Hell's Angels? Come on, Dev."

"You know what? Forget it." Dev grabbed his towel and unzipped the front of his tent. Crawling in, Dev untied his sleeping bag and rolled it out to lay on top of. Kicking off his shoes, he closed his eyes, still using the damp towel as a pillow. He could hear movement outside his tent. Imagining Sam crawling into his own private little cave, Dev was so wound up he knew he wouldn't sleep. Taking the rubber out of his short's pocket, he flipped it like a coin and it landed in the corner. Closing his eyes, he tried to forget everything and rest. His body was aching.

~

The sound of a zipper woke him. Opening his eyes, seeing it was almost pitch dark, Dev rubbed his face and looked at the foot of his tent. A figure was making its way inside his tiny domed canvas room which he knew had to be Sam. The flap closed again. Dev heard breathing in the small space. Not moving, nor saying a word, Dev waited, his heart pounding.

Hands felt their way in the darkness. One rode up Dev's calf to his thigh. The minute Sam made contact on Dev's skin, Dev's body reacted. Wanting this from the first moment he had laid eyes on Sam, Dev held back, holding his breath to see exactly what this fantastic leather rider was intending on doing to him.

When Sam figured out where Dev was in the tent, he managed to lie next to him. Without a word, Sam found Dev's shoulder, smoothing his fingers behind Dev's head. Urged from behind, Dev was drawn to Sam's lips. At the touch of his mouth and Sam's aggressive tongue, Dev went wild. Wrapping around Sam's back, Dev rolled on top of him, straddling Sam's hips and rushing his hands all over him. As Dev reached down, he couldn't believe Sam was naked. Immediately tilting off of him, Dev shed his shorts and resumed what he was doing, lying on top of Sam's body with his feet touching the sides of the small tent as he spread his legs wide over him. Sucking at his mouth, Dev moaned quietly, cupping Sam's rough jaw and grinding into Sam's cock under him. The kissing escalated with their writhing bodies. Dev felt the coarse scratching of Sam's shadow in ecstasy. It was just like he imagined it. Sam's taste, his scent, his movements, were turning Dev on so much he felt like he was already on the verge.

Sam's hands found Dev's ass, pushing him from behind, intensifying the friction. Between them sticky pre-come began to ooze and slide on their bellies. Through his clenched jaw, Dev hissed, "*Oh, Sam...you're amazing...*" as his craving to come grew extreme.

Sam parted their bodies.

Upset, needing to be wrapped around him, Dev waited, lying on his back, barely able to see a damn thing in the dark. Dev used his hands to keep tabs on where Sam was. A cock poked at Dev's face at the same time his own was devoured by a hot, wet mouth. Gripping the base of Sam's dick, Dev held back a grunt of pleasure with everything he had, knowing the sound could easily travel. Forcing himself to suck Sam's cock though all he wanted to do was lay back and savor his own blowjob, Dev slid that large penis into his mouth and devoured it. The sheer size of Sam's organ brought Dev to an altered state. It was thick and long, engorged to the point of exploding. Wrapping his lips around the head, tasting the salty drop on his tongue, Dev inhaled Sam's musky scent, mixed with the spicy soap he had used in the shower and moaned in delirium. Wishing he could see Sam's body in the darkness, admire his ass and balls from this wonderful angle, Dev closed his eyes and imagined it as his cock was fully immersed inside Sam's hot mouth. The suction was strong and the speed in which Sam moved became so arousing, Dev almost bit Sam's cock as he felt the orgasm in himself rise. He'd been so pent up, so ready for them to be doing this, Dev had to pause in his sucking because the rush to his loins became too intense to ignore.

Bending his knees, pushing his hips up into Sam's mouth, Dev came, clamping his eyes shut tight, keeping Sam's cock still in his mouth until the powerful sensations subsided. Obviously Sam was having trouble holding back, and his own hips began thrusting. Dev clasped both his hands around the base of Sam's cock and sucked like mad, fast and deep wanting to taste his come, craving it. Sam's organ rippled and hardened, filling Dev's entire mouth. A blast of come hit the back of his tongue. Dev swallowed him down, groaning softly.

Lapping at him gently, feeling Sam doing the same, Dev caught his breath and allowed Sam's cock to slip out of his mouth. In the pitch dark, Dev gave a good feel of Sam's balls and ass, knowing damn well he would drive him nuts for the rest of the trip. "You are so fucking amazing," Dev whispered as he assessed the size and shape of Sam's anatomy.

"Keep that up and I'll need to come again," came a quiet hiss.

"Get over here."

Sam managed to turn around in the tight space. Dev embraced him, allowing Sam to rest on top of him, and located his mouth. Kissing, running his hands through Sam's hair, Dev didn't want to stop. They were kindred spirits in so many ways. The motorcycle they chose, the fact that they were both self-employed, lived in a condo, it was kismet, and it was perfect. Loving the way Sam kissed, the soft lingering connection of their lips, and the deep passionate sucking and tongue swirling, Dev was already in heat for his second round. Pausing to catch his breath, Dev cupped Sam's face trying to make out his features in the darkness. Cuddling him close, nestled into Sam's fragrant hair, Dev wrapped around him with his legs and arms, wanting him to merge into his body.

Their rehardened cocks rested alongside each other in a warm dewy sweat that was driving Dev insane. "I could do this all night." Dev kissed Sam's face, his neck, moving to his ear to growl softly, showing his attraction.

Sam stroked Dev's back, gently, lovingly, in a calm affectionate way that Dev had never experienced from a lover before. It was as if Sam's sincerity and kindness were being broadcast in his touch.

Feeling the excitement in him stirring once more, Dev went for Sam's mouth, sucking it gently, fucking it with his tongue.

A low, rumbling laugh emerged from Sam.

Dev dug between them to get at their cocks. Holding them together, he gave them both a long slow stroke.

"Again?" Sam chuckled.

"And again, and again…" Dev tightened his grip, feeling his cock throb against Sam's.

"What the hell time is it?"

"Who cares?" Dev licked at Sam's chin.

"I should be getting back to my tent soon."

"No…" Dev moaned. "Not yet."

"I can't fall asleep here. And to be honest, Dev, I'm too tired to come again. I'm wiped out."

Considerate of Sam's wishes, Dev acquiesced.

"Do you want me to jerk you off again quickly?"

"No. It's okay. I'm exhausted too. You just turn me on…a lot." Dev kissed him.

"Good. Goodnight, Dev, you hot fucker."

Chuckling, Dev replied, "'Til we meet again?"

"Definitely."

Movement and the sound of a zipper followed. Dev imagined Sam crouching down naked in the dark and smiled. "Knew you were gay." He grinned in complete satisfaction, rolled over, and fell instantly back to sleep.

Chapter Four

There was so much noise of cars and shouting people, Dev woke from his dream. As he lay awake, he remembered last night and smiled wickedly. A week at Sturgis with a hot sexy hunk to enjoy. It was better than he could have hoped. He wanted to rush to Sam's tent and hug him he was so excited.

Checking his watch, he sat up, slipped his shorts on and unzipped his tent. Even though it was just nearing seven, the amount of traffic coming and going to the restroom and leaving the park was amazing. It was time to get a move on. Standing, his towel over his shoulder and his kit in his hand, Dev knelt by Sam's tent and called out his name in a hoarse whisper, "Sam? Baby? You up?"

Scratching his fingernails on the vinyl tent material, Dev asked louder. A low groan replied. A big smile on his face, Dev announced, "Time to get up, sleepyhead." About to say something provocative about last night, Dev paused at a noise of a condescending snort behind him.

"I'm surprised you two aren't waking up in the same tent together."

His good mood evaporating, Dev stood tall and confronted Tony. "What the fuck is your problem?"

Tony looked down his nose at Dev, his lip a constant sneer. "I hate queers."

"From my experience the assholes who hate queers the most are closet gays."

Tony reacted violently.

Dev dropped what he was holding and they grappled roughly. Tony had his hands on Dev's shoulders, shoving him back as Dev gripped Tony's forearms to get him off.

"All right!" Sam shoved between them, looking like he certainly had just rolled out a tent sleeping bag. "Jesus! You two are pathetic!"

Dev's chest heaving with anger, snarling in fury, he sneered, "Do me a favor, don't stay at our campground, you fucking moron."

"I tried to get out of it, asshole!" Tony shouted, "But everyone's booked. You think I want to be anywhere near you two faggots?"

Dev caught Sam spinning around to assess the surroundings. Several people heard and were staring. In rage, Dev went for Tony again, wanting to strangle him.

"I said stop!" Sam wedged between them and separated them roughly. "Get lost!" he warned Tony. "Or I'll let him beat the crap out of you."

"Like he could." Tony brushed his arms off. "No faggot is going to fucking beat me."

As he walked away Sam gave Dev an exasperated look. "Why do you sink to his level?"

"You think I'm going to sit here and take it? Oh man, you don't know me at all."

Sam held Dev's shoulders and looked him straight in the eye. "Listen to me." Sam appeared as furious as Dev felt. "There are five hundred thousand bikers at Sturgis. Are you following my logic here?"

Dev hated what he was about to say.

"What percentage of those hog-riders do you think are gay sympathizers? Huh, Dev? I'll fucking tell you. None! Zero! Even if the fuckers secretly jerk off to gay porn, they'd sooner kill us than act like they care."

Hearing the same lecture his dad had given him, Dev lowered his eyes in defeat.

"I don't know about you, Dev, but I want to come home alive and without fucking stitches." Sam released his hold on him. After another look around, Sam added, "Just cool it. Okay?"

Rubbing his face in anguish, Dev reached to gather his towel and kit. "I just wanted to tell you how fantastic last night was. I imagined a morning cuddle. Is that a crime?"

Sam gave Dev a sad smile. "No. And I appreciate the sentiment. I thought it was pretty amazing as well."

"Better." Dev whispered, "Can I kiss you in gratitude?"

"No."

His smile dropping, Dev turned aside and headed to the bathroom. Feeling Sam's gaze on his profile, Dev hated hiding, *hated it*!

~

Though the air temperature was above eighty, Dev was wearing his leathers and helmet. Seeing Tony and Ralph riding behind Jerry and his wife June, dressed in shorts and a T-shirt, sans helmet, Dev felt like everywhere he looked someone was rubbing his face in it. Whatever *it* was.

By his side, already the steadfast friend, not to mention, secret lover, Sam had his entire leather outfit on as well, and was wiping the sweat off his face before he flipped down his visor. The journey was a simple straight shot down Interstate 90 to Rapid City. Three hundred miles of tarmac lay between them and absolute insanity. Dev was both dreading and craving it simultaneously. *Christ, I wish Dad was here*. His father was a tough SOB who no one messed with. No, Jan Young wasn't huge, but he was crazy. He remembered someone saying his dad had "mad eyes". Well, no, he didn't think his father had mad eyes, until, that is, he got mad. Jan was the kind of guy who would go completely ballistic in a fight. Dev had heard the war stories from his mom. The details were gruesome. Dev supposed if you were going to win, you had to fight like a wildcat. Perhaps that was now Dev's motto. He certainly wasn't afraid to be himself and the fact that Sam was, gnawed at him.

His stomach grumbling from only consuming a granola bar and instant coffee from a vending machine, Dev wanted a full meal and a chance to unwind. But that had to wait three hundred ass-vibrating miles.

With Sam once again by his side and the column of bikes stretching out before and behind them, Dev couldn't stop his mind from racing. Bouncing between having Sam's fantastic cock in his mouth, to Tony's threats and homophobic attitude, Dev was torn in two as to how to enjoy himself at this ultimate biker's rally. What he wanted to do was to feel at ease to show Sam his attention, to sleep together if they chose. What he did not want to do was watch the stupid biker girl competitions and pretend to drool over tits and ass.

A large bug hit his helmet face screen and ricocheted to his neck. Wincing at the sting, Dev pulled his zipper higher up his throat and hoped good old Tony and Ralph were enjoying the bug battering with their macho, *I don't need leathers* attitude.

Peeking at Sam as he rode next to him, Dev moaned. *Oh, Sam...just let it go and be out in public with me.*

He felt heartsick, but wondered if perhaps his father and Sam were showing more common sense than he was. Life wasn't fair. No shit.

~

Four hours later they finally exited the interstate into Rapid City. The amount of motorcycles in the area was already beyond belief. As they slowed down on the ramp, Dev was dying to ask Sam what he thought. Dev knew what to expect, his adorable friend didn't. For a much needed break, Jerry and June had them all gather in a dirt lot near the main street. Pulling off his helmet, Dev felt the warm air on his sweaty head.

"Okay, boys and girls!" Jerry smiled. "Here we are. I take it some of you want to go to the campsites or hotels to freshen up or grab a bite, others are dying to see Mount Rushmore and the Blackhills, and maybe a few of you just want to keep riding to Sturgis right now. Either way, I don't want to stop you."

Doug shouted, "Aren't we all staying at Buffalo Chip?"

Jerry acknowledged him. "Well, let's be honest, it's where the damn party is." He laughed. "I'm at a cabin there with the Mrs.," he pointed to his wife who was seated behind him on his bike, "but I'm sure as heck am going to join you campers for all of the events."

Ralph shouted, "We have our mobile phone list. Why don't we go our separate ways and meet up somewhere inside Buffalo for dinner?"

"Good idea." Jerry checked his watch. "How about seven thirty we all call each other and pick a spot. It won't be easy. That's the biggest campground of the lot, but there are landmarks. Just get it straight where you'd like to meet up." Putting his helmet back on, Jerry waved, "It was great riding with you all so far. Catch ya in a bit!" He took off with five other old-timers.

Dev scowled at Tony who appeared to want to be the "leader" of the pack as he waved the rest closer so he could be heard.

"I'm already hating this," Dev snarled.

Sam admonished, "Just go with it, Dev."

Rolling closer to the circle of riders, Dev heard Tony shouting, "We can ride to the campsite now, check in, and then decide on where to meet later."

Ralph added, "I know there's a Domino's there. Why don't we meet there at seven, seven thirty?"

Everyone seemed to agree. Dev put his helmet on and muttered to Sam, "Let's go."

"To the campground?"

"No. I'd like to find a café first and eat. I'm so fucking hungry I feel lightheaded."

"Lead the way." Sam flipped his visor down.

Looking back, Dev noticed a few of the new sub-group watched them go. He could imagine Tony making the excuse, "They're gay, we don't want them with us anyhow."

Slowing up when he spotted a café right on the main street, Dev parked his bike alongside several hundred others, and took off his helmet. Sam did the same next to him.

"Christ, I'm roasting." Sam wiped at his dripping face.

"What have you got on under the leather pants?"

"Nothing!" Sam tried to laugh.

"Then don't strip."

"You?"

"Briefs. Christ, Sam, nothing? You trying to get me horny or yourself chafed?"

"Both?" He smiled.

Dev unzipped his jacket, finding his shirt soaked with sweat under it. Taking his jacket off, knowing he had to carry it because his saddlebags were overflowing, he held it and his helmet and managed to get off the bike without tripping and falling. His legs were still vibrating and numb from the ride.

Once Sam was standing beside him, jacket and helmet in hand, he whistled, "Jesus Christ, look at all these bikes!"

"This is nothing. Wait 'til we get to Sturgis. There are so many of them, you can't believe what you're seeing."

"It's fucking hot, but at least there's a breeze."

Dev watched Sam unstick his wet white T-shirt from his skin. His nipples showed through the cotton and were erect. "Stop that. You have any idea how much I want to suck on your fucking hard nipples?"

"Behave," Sam chided.

"Yeah, yeah, whatever." Tearing his eyes away from Sam's distracting body, Dev entered the café and unfortunately found it packed, like every other place from here on would be. "Shit."

"Don't worry. Look, there's someone leaving."

Pausing as the couple stood, placed a tip on the table and left, Dev made his way to the two chairs. A busboy noticed and came over to clear it off.

"Thanks." Dev smiled at him.

"No problem."

Draping his leather jacket on the back of the chair and placing his helmet on the floor by the table legs, Dev dropped down and moaned. "My poor ass."

He heard a chuckle behind him and spun around. An older man with a bandana and gray beard smiled in agreement. "Bet you're riding a Jap-bike."

"How'd you guess?" Dev replied amiably.

"Because if ya had a chopper, your ass wouldn't be as sore."

"Maybe. But I'd have motor oil all over my leathers." Dev winked at him and was glad he laughed at the joke.

Turning back to Sam, he caught his adoring grin. "Yes?" Dev chuckled.

"I am so glad you're with me."

"And I can't wait for that ass rub," Dev whispered over the metal napkin dispenser that was in the middle of the table. "And to suck you again."

Sam looked around in paranoia.

"What can I get you boys?" The waitress held up her pad and pencil.

Dev looked over the menu quickly while he had her attention in the busy room.

Beginning before him, Sam requested, "I'll have the gold-panner's special, side of fries and ice water, please."

Trying to find the item on the menu, Dev closed it and said, "The same." He handed her the two menus and she left.

"Rapid City," Sam announced as if he were surprised.

"Yeah, well, it's not New York."

"It's not even Centerville. It's like a pretend cowboy set from an old Fifties television show."

The waitress returned with their ice water, leaving again.

They both chugged it down to the bottom.

Dev set his empty glass down and looked around at the crowd. Leaning across the table, he said quietly, "This is pretty much a microcosm of what you can expect at the event."

Sam sat up and had a discreet peek at the clientele.

Men with worn denim vests, torn at the sleeves, biker patches on the back, shaved heads, beards, tattoos, Fry boots, chains, leather pants, and beer.

"Yup," Sam replied, "exactly what I pictured."

"I'll tell you a secret. Even some of the guys who look like that?" Dev tilted his head to another table, "Are professional businessmen like the guys in our group. I think they live out some mid-life fantasy here. You know?"

"Well, Christ, Dev, look at the line up of entertainment. Alice Cooper? Lynyrd Skynyrd? They're old men from the Seventies who still play. I didn't expect too many young guys."

"It's a mix. Honest it is."

A plate of gold-panner's grub showed up which consisted of a bacon cheeseburger, coleslaw, and a side of fries. The waitress set a bottle of ketchup down. "Will there be anything else?"

"More water, thanks." Sam smiled at her.

She winked in reply and set their check down against the napkin dispenser.

As Dev shoved a fry in his mouth, he moaned. "Christ, I am so hungry."

Before Sam answered he watched the waitress fill their glasses from an iced pitcher. "Thank you."

"My pleasure." She walked away.

"Anyway," Sam continued, "me too. I expected us to stop for breakfast first thing this morning. I was surprised Jerry just got us on the road."

"Well, I think he just wanted us to get here." Dev was demolishing his burger so fast he was hardly chewing.

"So, what's this Buffalo Chip place like?"

"Woodstock, times five."

Sam stopped chewing. "No."

Nodding to enforce his answer while he was still chewing, when Dev swallowed he said, "I swear, it's a mini Sodom and Gomorra. Luckily it's well organized."

"I bet it's insane."

"It is. Lots of naked drunk people doing naked drunk things."

"Naked men?" Sam whispered softly.

"Some. Mostly chicks. And mostly chicks that should never be caught naked." Dev gulped his water to wash down the burger.

"Ew…" Sam curled his nose.

"You'll see." Dev shoved his french fries into his mouth two by two.

Once they had eaten and taken a piss break, they stood next to their bikes to debate their next move.

"When would you like to see some sights?" Dev asked. "You do realize Mount Rushmore is only a few miles from here."

"I'm too beat for more riding."

Laughing, Dev asked, "How are you expecting to get to the campsite? Walk?"

"No. I mean extra riding. Can we save Mount Rushmore for tomorrow?'

"Of course. You want to go get checked in and chill?"

Putting his jacket back on, Sam answered, "If you can chill with half a million people hanging around."

"You can. Once we're away from the masses that will be hanging around the vendors' booths and food court and get to the campsite, it is less hectic." Dev put his helmet on pausing to look at the bugs. "Jesus! You know, one hit my fucking throat." He pulled the neck of his T-shirt down. "Am I bruised?"

Sam leaned closer. "You do have a red mark. Looks like a hickey."

"Kiss it to make it better?"

"You never stop."

"No. I won't. Get used to it." Dev slipped his jacket back on. Just sitting back on the seat made Dev wince. "Oh, my poor nuts!"

A few Harley riders laughed at him as they walked passed. Before he said something to instigate a fight, Dev bit his lip and started the engine.

Finding their way to the campground and waiting on line to check in, Dev and Sam moved inch by inch as the attendants checked IDs and searched packages for contraband. Finally at the main gate, Dev handed the man his driver's license and credit card.

"One tent?"

"Yes."

"Five days?"

"Yes again."

He was given a plastic ID bracelet, which he slipped on, and paperwork. He signed his credit card slip and retrieved his driver's license.

"Are you with the Leather Boys?"

"Yes, why? Do you have us on a list?"

"I do. Someone before you gave us a list of members and it's also on our computer."

"Oh."

"They should be in this area here." The man circled a spot on a map of the park. "It's all on a first come first serve basis with the tents, so you may want to set up now."

"Okay, thanks." Dev folded the paperwork and stuffed it into his jacket.

As he waited for Sam to do the same, he looked at the number of bikes and campervans waiting to get in. The place was already mobbed.

Once Sam had finished, he rolled up next to Dev with his map. "I think it's that way."

"Tony will be there."

"So what? Just stay the hell away from him." Sam placed his helmet on his head but kept his visor up.

Slowly they made their way around the crowd to the outlying areas, passed the campervans and pop-up trailers into a virtual city of small canvas tents.

"It's already filling up." Sam kept moving to the nearest clearing. "I hope to hell that's a toilet and shower."

When they stopped, Dev pulled out his map to orient himself. "It is."

"The good thing is if we're this close, we have easy access. The bad thing is everyone will be tramping through us at night to get to it."

"How about over there?" Dev pointed away from the actually building area.

"Better." Sam hit the accelerator and rode over to the grassy spot. Shutting off the engine, swinging his leg over it, Sam immediately took off his helmet and jacket, setting them on the seat of his bike.

As Dev twisted his key to silence the motor and climbed off, he stripped from the wait up, using his T-shirt to wipe his sweaty face. "I have to get out of these leathers."

"Ditto."

Untying the pup tent, Dev set it up quickly and dove into it to change. His legs were sticking to the leather he was so overheated. Wearing just his gym shorts, he climbed back out and looked for Sam. He could see his shadow inside his own tent. Dev imagined him naked, instantly salivating at another chance to get at his cock.

While he waited he tried to find anyone from their group. Since they weren't assigned spaces, he imagined it might be more of a challenge than he anticipated. Which, again, might be a good thing.

Glimpsing Sam's tight ass as it poked out of his tent, Dev gaped at it in awe. His shorts were short, *very short*. From his vantage point Dev could see Sam's balls through the material, for they were the only thing covered from the back at the moment. Sam's fantastic butt cheeks were exposed.

Growing hard and having the urge to kneel down and lick his ass, it took every ounce of willpower Dev had to not take advantage of the situation, knowing Sam's reluctance to be open about their attraction.

Looking around quickly, Dev stood in front of him, protecting him from prying eyes. "You almost done?"

"Yes. Why?"

"Because your absolutely fantastic ass is hanging out, dear."

"Shit!" Sam climbed out and adjusted his shorts to cover better.

Dev had to conceal his smile. "Sorry. Though I was enjoying it, I had a feeling you hadn't intended on mooning the crowd. At least not until you've had a few."

The red color in Sam's cheeks was priceless. "It's just that it's so fucking hot I don't want to put my jeans on yet."

"Hey! I'm not complaining."

Throwing a towel on the grass near their tents, Sam dropped down and lay flat.

"Back killing you?" Dev sat next to him.

"Yes. I'm dying."

"Will you let me help?"

"Later."

"So, I can't even rub your lower back?"

"Here? Fuck no."

Sitting up, getting annoyed, Dev wrapped his arms around his stiff knees as he looked around the area. "You realize no one gives a shit."

"They would if you were planted on my ass rubbing me."

"Why are you so afraid?"

Raising his head up, Sam gave Dev an exasperated look.

"Fine. Suffer."

"Thank you."

Digging his own towel out of his saddlebag, along with the two bottles of water they had bought, which were warm at the moment, Dev spread his towel out next to Sam and set the bottles down between them. Lying on his stomach, Dev rested his head on his arms, staring at Sam's profile. "Do you have an agenda for tonight?"

"Yes. Stay the hell off my bike and not sit on my ass."

Dev chuckled. "You want an aspirin?"

"I want a glute massage."

"I offered."

"Later." After a yawn, Sam muttered, "I need a nap.

Motivating himself up again, Dev pulled some paperwork out of his saddlebag and dropped back down next to a weary Sam. Flipping pages Dev read, "Right, six thirty to seven there's some bike stunt riding. Uh, seven to seven thirty, a rodeo...ooh, cowboys? I'd like to see some cowboys. Says here they're doing some kind of rodeo shit, something like that. We'll skip the girl wrestlers I assume...oh, and we're supposed to meet everyone at Domino's Pizza at seven."

"I'm dyin'."

Blowing out a breath in exasperation, Dev said, "Will you just get in your tent and let me massage your ass?"

"Someone will see us and kill us."

"Then shut the fuck up." Dev read through the pamphlet again, opened a bottle of water and swigged it down. "When the hell's Alice Cooper on? Shit, we missed him. He was here last Sunday. Well, that sucks." Seeing Sam crawling to his tent, Dev shook his head sadly. After he unzipped it and disappeared, Dev made sure all their valuables were hidden inside the tents, including their leather jackets and helmets. One more look at the oblivious crowd and he crept into Sam's tent, closing the zipper.

"All right, you poor thing." Dev sat next to him. While Sam lay on his stomach, his head resting on his arms, Dev began rubbing his bottom over his gym shorts.

"Augh, God! I can't believe how sore I am."

"I know. Just relax."

Sam spread his legs so his toes touched the corners of the small tent.

Getting more comfortably seated, Dev reached over Sam and massaged his lower back, butt, and upper legs.

A soft whimper came out of Sam as Dev tried to be gentle yet firm. Reaching between Sam's thighs, Dev rubbed the base of his balls, where he himself was sore.

Sam moaned, "I'd be turned on if I wasn't so achy."

"I know, babe."

"I envy those choppers. They sit reclining with a backrest. Look at us. Leaning over those fucking crotch-rockets like ten-speed racers."

"They're not the perfect bikes for touring. We know that."

"Then why did we use them as touring bikes?"

"Because we're insane?" Dev chuckled, digging his fingers deeper into the flesh of Sam's ass cheeks. "Christ, you may be too sore to be hot, but I'm making my pants wet." Dev peeked down at his blue gym shorts and found a small seeping stain. "Sam, I am so hot for your bod, I'm dyin' here."

"Later. In the dark."

"What do you think people are doing out there? Leaning their ears against the canvas of our tent?" Dev slipped his hand into the back of Sam's shorts, rubbing skin on skin.

"Christ, that feels fantastic. Do you know how to massage people?"

"Like, have I been taught?" Dev asked.

"Yes."

"No. Not formally. My ex-wife and I used to exchange them on occasion."

"It feels professional."

Chuckling, Dev asked, "Yeah? You ever have a massage therapist do this?" He pushed his finger against Sam's anus, growing rock hard at the gesture.

"Funny."

Rubbing Sam in silence for a few minutes, Dev sighed. "I want to eat you. You have an amazing body."

"I noticed that about you. Especially last night. Nice cock."

"Thanks." Dev adjusted his position to straddle Sam's thighs for better access at rubbing his back, up his spine to his shoulders.

"Keep that up and I'll fall in love."

Dev laughed softly. "It'd be better with oil."

"Always is."

"I meant the rub."

"I didn't."

Dev kept going, massaging Sam's arms and neck knowing how good it would feel to get one himself. His cock was poking at the front of his gym shorts and the damp spot was spreading. "You asleep? Because if you are, I'm going to slip my cock inside your ass."

"Close. Oh, man...could you go back to my butt? It's the worst part of me."

"Oh contraire."

"I mean the most sore."

Climbing off Sam's thighs, Dev sat next to him again and kneaded his ass and balls.

"I am so tender between my fucking legs. I feel like I need to sit on a fucking doughnut cushion for a few days to give my testicles a break."

Dev reached back inside Sam's shorts, between his thighs to that spot. Gently caressing it, Dev was so excited he wished he could jerk off. "I can do it with my tongue."

"Later."

"You're a fucking cock-tease, Rhodes."

"I know. Suffer."

"I am, believe me." Dev pushed at his hard-on to try and stop it from throbbing. It only made it seep more sticky fluid. "There. Hold you for now?" Dev removed his hand from Sam's shorts, going completely mad for him and struggling to not cross the imaginary line Sam had drawn.

Sam rolled over stiffly and groaned. After a minute he observed the dampness of Dev's shorts. "Jesus, Dev."

"I know. What can I say? You excite me."

"How's your ass?"

"Aching for your dick."

"Later. I mean is it sore?"

"Fuck yeah. You kidding me? We ride the same damn bike."

"You're not complaining as much as I am."

"Should I?"

"Lie down."

Dev exchanged places with Sam. Reaching into his shorts, Dev set his erect cock upright first and relaxed, face down on Sam's sleeping bag, his hands propped under his head.

At the first touch of Sam's hands on his raw bottom, Dev flinched.

"No good?"

"No. It's good. I just am a little surprised at how painful it is."

"I know."

Dev closed his eyes. Sam was kneading his ass cheeks and it felt *so* incredible he was about to cry. "I should just buy a Harley."

"Bite your tongue."

"Well? You think they all have sore fucking balls?" As he said it, Sam's hand reached between his thighs. In reflex Dev spread his legs. Sam caressed the back of his testicles and Dev cringed in both pain and pleasure. "Sure would feel better with your tongue."

"Later!"

"Okay! Geez. Your paranoia is killing me."

"No. The homophobes will kill you. Not me."

"Christ, that's fantastic."

"I can't believe how much more riding we have to do."

"As little or as much as you want, babe."

"I want a car."

"Now you sound like a wimp." Dev laughed. Sam finally dipped his hand into Dev's shorts. "'Bout time."

"You're already getting come all over yourself."

"That's my problem." Dev moaned as Sam's hand found his tender spots and lightly caressed them. "Oh, yes. Right there."

"Same exact place as me."

"Same exact anatomy and bike as you, pretty boy."

"Right there?"

Dev flinched involuntarily. "Right there." Feeling his cock throbbing like crazy, Dev began pumping his hips against the ground.

"What are you doing?"

"Fucking your sleeping bag because you won't let me fuck you."

"Why can't you wait?"

Dev rolled over quickly, causing Sam's hand to get trapped in his shorts and under his butt. "Because! Okay?"

"Shh!" Sam wrestled his hand out of Dev's clothing. "Isn't this bad enough?"

"Bad?" Dev was about to explode. He unzipped the front of the tent and climbed out. When he stood up, Tony and Ralph were just passing.

"Shit." Dev met their eyes instantly. In reflex, Dev covered his crotch.

Since he and Ralph hadn't crossed swords yet, Ralph smiled. "Dev! We're all right down there." Ralph pointed a few yards away at a cluster of tents. "Jerry and the gang are going to see the Patriot Riders at four. Are you guys thinking of going?"

Dev couldn't help but connect to Tony's suspicious gaze. "I don't know."

"Where's Sam?" Tony scoffed.

Dev hoped to hell he didn't climb out of his tent at that moment. "Uh, men's room."

"So? You'll come by?" Ralph asked.

"We'll try."

"Cool. Hopefully we'll see ya in a few."

As they walked away Tony looked back over his shoulder at him. Dev returned his sneer of contempt.

After they had left, Dev moved his hands and looked down at himself. Well, his hard-on had definitely vanished, but the small stain was still present.

A hoarse whisper asked, "They gone?"

"Yes."

Sam climbed out and looked around. "Shit. See?" he accused.

"Shut up." Dev was tired of the closet act.

"We weren't even doing anything and we could have been caught."

"Caught doing what?" Dev moaned. "Never mind. You do what you like, Sam. I'm sick of the games." Dev crawled into his own tent and tried to rest. When he curled up on his sleeping bag he smelled Sam's scent on his hands. Inhaling them deeply, he sighed in frustration and closed his eyes.

Chapter Five

"Dev?"

Feeling groggy and hot, Dev tried to wake up.

"You in there?"

"Yes." Dev checked his watch.

"You interested in watching the Patriot Riders and getting some food?"

Opening the zipper of the tent, Dev found Sam in a pair of tight faded jeans, torn at the right knee and left thigh, and his Leather Boys T-shirt.

"Wow."

"Behave," Sam admonished, tongue in cheek, wagging his finger at him.

Inching his way out of the tent, Dev stood, stretching his back. "Don't ask me to behave when you look that good, okay? Right. Clothes." He used his key to open his saddlebag, removing the same outfit, jeans and the group T-shirt. "Be a sec."

"I'll be waiting."

Taking a last look at Sam's amazing body, Dev crawled back inside his tent and changed wanting them to have a quick shared orgasm before they left, and knowing they couldn't.

~

Sam relaxed against his bike, watching the crowd coming and going around him. It was warm but very breezy and he anticipated as the night drew closer the air temperature would drop. His gaze back on the tent and the silhouetted movement inside, Sam imagined Dev getting dressed in the tight space. It'd been almost a year since his last relationship. He'd been hesitant to get into another. Being burned did that to a man.

But Dev was fun, confident, and adorable. In some ways Sam wished they were at a Gay Pride event. This was anything but. Though he craved to play and flirt openly, Sam was scared to death to do it here.

When the zipper unraveled and the front flap fell back, Sam anticipated handsome Dev Young in his jeans and T-shirt. "Look at you. Nice. We match." Sam grinned wickedly as they stood close.

"Hopefully everyone else is wearing theirs."

"Why?"

"I don't know." Dev knelt down by his bike and opened another compartment.

When he took out a heavy chain, Sam was surprised. "You locking it up?"

"Yes. To yours. Bring it over here next to mine."

Sam reacted quickly, rolling his motorcycle alongside Dev's. Dev slid the heavy chain through the front wheels, locking them together.

"Not a lot we can do about our leather gear and helmets," Sam mused.

"No, but they're not nearly as expensive to replace."

"Do bikes get stolen here?"

"My dad said it does happen. He's the one who recommended the lock." Dev stood tall, looking over at their bikes wistfully.

While Sam waited, Dev dug through his saddlebag, producing a digital camera. "You know, I have an idea."

"What's that?"

"I'm going to take my street clothes out, stick it in the tent and lock up my leathers. No one will steal my fucking underwear."

"I would." Sam winked.

"Pervert."

"You have no idea." Agreeing with his thoughts, Sam did the same, taking out his inexpensive toiletries and clothes, tossing them inside his tent, and crushing his leather outfit into the empty space.

"Do you mean I have no idea how perverted you are? Did I find a good one?" Dev's blue eyes sparkled mischievously.

"I don't know if I'm good, but I can be wicked." Sam was glad it made Dev smile.

After Dev patted his back pocket where his wallet was, he tucked his key into his pants and sighed. "I was hoping you would prove it to me at this event, but, oh well." He tried not to catch Sam's gaze. "Best we can do. If our helmets and toothbrushes get stolen, tough."

"It'll be all right."

They walked to where the Patriot Riders were supposed to do their thing. Passing a food court, Dev nudged Sam. "How about a beer and a snack first?"

"Sounds good." Sam followed Dev to a bar.

Waiting in the line, Sam brushed Dev's shoulder as he ordered two beers from the tap. After handing Sam a cold frosty mug, Dev asked, "Chips?"

Leaning against him to look over the snacks, Sam replied, "Yeah, how about the mesquite ones."

"Two bags of mesquite potato chips as well," Dev relayed to the bartender.

When Sam offered Dev money his hand was pushed back. "Come on. Dutch."

"You get the pizza."

"Okay." Sam sipped the beer.

After Dev gave him his bag of chips, Dev made a move to touch Sam's face. "What?" Sam flinched back.

"You have a foam mustache, that's all."

Wiping it off himself, Sam looked around in suspicion.

"Christ, Sam!" Dev remonstrated. "Then stop rubbing up against me so much."

"Shut up," Sam hissed in anxiety.

Looking around for a place to sit, Sam found a picnic table with a small open gap in the bodies. He stood near it and asked, "Anyone sitting here?"

The husky biker gave Sam a once over. "No."

"Thanks." Sam sat down, resting his beer on the table. Dev squeezed into the tiny space next to him.

"Leather Boys? What are you riding?" the biker asked.

"Kawasakis." Sam pulled open the bag of potato chips and began eating.

"How far did you ride?"

"From fucking Dayton," Dev moaned, leaning over Sam to speak to the man.

"Long haul on a crotch-rocket."

"Yes. My ass is trashed." Sam took another sip of beer.

"Hell, at least you rode. Some of the non-Harley riders end up either trailering it, or renting one here. That isn't right in my book. It's about the ride."

"That's what my friend tells me." Sam gestured to Dev. "He's been here before."

"Oh? You a Sturgis virgin?" The man appeared amused.

"Unfortunately."

The biker leaned around Sam to ask Dev, "You warn him?"

"I've tried."

Sam watched Dev lick the salt off his fingers. "I know it'll be wild."

"Wait 'til nightfall when the beer flows more liberally. You'll see it all," the man said.

"It's so hard not to get distracted here and forget you're not actually at Sturgis." Sam drank more beer after he finished his chips.

"Most of the big events are here. But you should take a drive through. Go on a tour."

"On my bike again? On this sore ass?" Sam laughed at the absurdity.

"Find a nice biker-chick and hop on the back of her Harley."

Giving the man a fake smile, Sam replied, "Good idea."

"They got all sorts of contests here later. Ones sponsored by the place, others not."

At the wicked grin he was getting from the man, Sam turned to look back at Dev.

Dev's expression reflected the biker's. "Women."

"Oh." Sam nodded.

"If ya like tits, you'll see plenty of them." The man wiped the beer off his handlebar mustache.

"Oh. Good." Sam tried to appear enthused. "Uh, you ready?" he asked Dev. He was tired of pretending as well, but that was life.

Looking slightly surprised at the sudden rush, Dev sucked down his beer, crushed up his empty potato chip bag and stood.

"Nice chatting with you." Sam smiled at the man.

"You too. Have fun."

While they dumped their garbage, Sam mumbled to Dev, "Naked women, goody goody."

"It's why all the boys come here, Sam-sweetie."

"I thought it was for the bikes."

"Oh, you have much to learn, grasshopper."

"Then why the hell are you here?" Sam paused to stare at him.

"Hey, I don't mind women. I married one, remember?" Dev urged him to keep walking.

"You're bi?" Sam asked in agony.

Looking around them as they proceeded through a very tight crowd, Dev replied, "Could you say that any louder? Sheesh!"

Sam didn't realize how crushed he felt. The last thing he needed was to compete with a woman for Dev's affection.

Moving passed vendors selling bike apparel, accessories, beef jerky, and leather everything, Sam felt Dev fall in behind him in single file until they moved beyond the congested mob. In his ear, Dev breathed, "No, I'm not bi." Then Dev patted Sam's bottom affectionately.

"Thank fuck!" Sam exhaled, hearing Dev's chuckle.

Finally beyond the tightly packed tunnel of bodies and through the other side, Sam was able to walk next to Dev once more. Yes, he did want to hold Dev's hand, but that didn't mean he would.

"Look up there."

Sam turned his head to the sky where Dev pointed. A dark army helicopter was circling. "What's that for?"

"Don't know."

They paused, watching as it flew overhead. Everyone seemed to stop to gaze up at it.

"Where were we?" Sam brought his attention back to Dev when chopper had left. Dev was staring at him intensely. "What? Aren't we going to see some Patriot Riding thing?"

"I want to kiss you so badly, I ache."

"Dev," Sam chided, gazing around. "Later."

"Christ, is that the only word you know?" Dev started moving again.

"No." Sam wanted to tell him another word he knew, much naughtier, but kept quiet.

"Shit. Look. That must be it."

Sam spun around to see. A flat grassy field was loaded with American flags and a huge crowd was gathering, many in army fatigues. "Wow. That's impressive."

"Let's get closer."

In the stiff warm breeze the flags whipped and shimmered. Sam instantly felt a lump in his throat. He'd always been very patriotic.

As they drew closer, Sam and Dev stood at a small information sign posted near a booth. "It says each flag represents a fallen hero," Sam explained.

Dev pressed against Sam from behind, reading over his shoulder. "Want to buy one? Help the cause?"

"Yes." Sam removed his wallet.

"Do you know a fallen hero?"

"My brother's in Iraq. I hope to hell I never hear about him 'falling'." He handed the man behind a table some money.

The man put it into a box. "Thank you."

Dev stuffed some cash into the collection jar.

A wave of sorrow overwhelmed Sam. As he walked closer to the sea of red, white, and blue, he dabbed at his eyes. Dev's arm wrapped around Sam's shoulders.

"All right. Don't worry."

"I hate him being over there."

"I know. It must suck."

Dev kissed Sam's hair.

"Dev, please." Sam nudged him back.

"Don't you think it's natural for people to comfort each other in a place like this?"

"Not with a kiss. No." Sam knew he was hurting Dev's feelings, but he didn't want any harassment.

Obviously insulted, Dev walked away.

"Dev…" Sam called after him. Pausing, he heard the sound of motorcycle engines and looked up over the crowd. A column of uniformed riders appeared. Watching them as he walked, Sam made his way over to Dev to enjoy the display. It was so touching, it kept making Sam well up with emotion.

~

After taking some photos, Dev knew Sam was on the verge of tears. Folding his arms over his chest, Dev watched the action on the field and could hear Sam choking up. "For cryin' out loud." He held onto Sam again, pulling him to his side. There were so many other people with tears running down their faces, Dev couldn't imagine anyone thinking badly of them. And there were men holding other men as well. Brothers in arms. Soldiers. Veterans. Straight men.

Peeking at Sam, seeing him fighting back the tears with everything he had, Dev smiled sweetly at him. Squeezing him tighter, Dev was savoring a man whose sensitivity and kindness were a pure virtue. Silently, Dev said a prayer to protect Sam's brother.

~

Once the show had ended and the crowd dispersed, Dev took out his event schedule. "Oh! Lady wrestlers next!"

"Groan." Sam attempted a smile.

"Could be amusing."

"No thanks."

"Then we have an hour before the stunt riders and an hour and a half before we meet the club members…wait a minute. We'll miss the rodeo."

"Can I see that?" Sam asked, looking over the event descriptions. "You realize it's not really cowboys. It says motorcycle riders and anyone can join in. Where did you get the idea it was cowboys? I thought you'd been here before."

"I was. But I was only a teen."

As Sam read over the entertainment, Dev moved to lean against him on the pretext of looking at it over his shoulder. "Christ, you smell divine."

"Don't get yourself into a state."

Although he said that, Dev noticed Sam didn't move away from his contact. "I'm perpetually horny with you around."

"Down, boy."

"Yeah, right."

When Dev snuck a light peck on Sam's neck, Sam bolted back and spun around in anger. Taking a terrified scan of their surroundings, Sam went pale.

Dev noticed some hostile sets of eyes as well. "Come on. Keep walking."

Folding the pamphlet, Sam snarled, "Why are you intent on getting us killed?"

"It's not my intention. So shut up."

"It will happen. I'm telling you if you don't cut it out, I'll be furious with you."

"Oh?" Dev stopped short and confronted him. "You know me all of three fucking days and you think I care what you think?"

"Fuck you."

When Sam turned to storm away, Dev grabbed him. "I'm lying. I care."

Exhaling in exasperation, Sam explained, "We have all the time in the world after this event. Why can't you just wait?"

"Because! I'm madly attracted to you, Sam, and I'm out."

"I'm out too. But not here!" Sam looked around again.

"That's hypocritical!"

"No, it's survival." Sam shoved him. "Shut up and keep moving. There's a motorcycle display somewhere around here."

"You know, by tomorrow I'm going to want to get out of this mob and cruise around."

"Me too, sore ass or not."

"Good. Have you ever seen Mount Rushmore? It's really amazing."

"No. I've only seen pictures of it."

"What the hell are we going to do now to kill a couple of hours? You know, we could screw."

Rolling his eyes at Dev's persistence, Sam offered, "There's the Harley tent. Let's at least look at some bikes."

"In our Leather Boy crotch-rocket T's? We'll get nothing but grief."

"They've been okay so far." Sam entered the tent and was drawn to the chopped out Harley on display. "Nice!"

"My dad had a hog like that. He bought it in the Seventies. Funny how it looks the same."

"How you boys doing today?"

They looked up at the salesman.

"Fine. Just admiring the machine." Sam gestured to the bike.

"What do you ride?"

"A Kawasaki."

"I see."

Dev rolled his eyes, waiting for the teasing.

"Did you ride it here?" the man asked.

"Yes, from Dayton."

"How's your ass?" the man laughed at Sam.

"Sore! All right?" Sam laughed back.

"Here we go!" Dev folded his arms over his chest.

"You too?" The man was hardly holding back his amusement.

"All right. We've already heard enough."

"And you got that ride all the way back." The man nudged his friend and they were both rolling with hilarity.

"Let's go, Sam." Dev wasn't in the mood.

"Nice chatting with you guys." Sam waved.

The men just kept laughing as they left. Dev shook his head. "If anyone asks, you ride a Harley Sportster from now on, okay?"

"I don't mind some gentle teasing, Dev. I just don't want a fat lip."

"Whatever."

Instinctively they returned to their tents. Other than drink, eat, or ogle lady wrestlers, there wasn't much else to do at the moment. Once they made it back to their spot, which had gotten congested as more and more people showed up with large canopy style tents, coolers, and gas grills, Dev dropped back to the grass and relaxed. "I could nap again. What the hell's wrong with me?"

"It's the heat. Also I think we're still recuperating from the ride here." Sam found a place next to him. "There's no shade anywhere. They have the right idea." Sam tilted his head to a group of young people with a large open gazebo tent.

"Bet they came in a truck."

"They had to. You can't fit that on a bike." Sam laid flat, his hands behind his head.

Looking down at him, Dev salivated at Sam's exposed abdomen that was revealed between the bottom edge of his shirt and the top of his tight torn jeans.

"Did you make those holes on purpose?" Gesturing to the gaping tears in Sam's denims, Dev wanted to stroke his skin but knew he'd get yelled at.

"No. They just wore through."

Lying on his side next to him, Dev asked quietly, "How long does your brother have to be in Iraq?"

"A year. He's due back around November."

"I feel really bad for you."

"Me? Feel bad for him."

"That's kind of what I meant." Dev had the urge to brush Sam's hair back from his forehead affectionately, but again, didn't.

"Hey, fellas!" Doug Allen sat down on the grass with them, wearing his T-shirt proudly.

"Hi, Doug!" Sam sat up and gave him a big smile.

"What have you men been up to?"

"We watched the Patriot Riders." Sam wrapped his arms around his knees as he spoke.

"Yes. So did we. Nice show. You heading over to the lady wrestlers?"

"We thought we'd take a break." Sam looked back at Dev.

Dev wasn't talking. He didn't feel like he had anything to contribute.

"Are you going to the biker rodeo or the stunt riders later?"

"Maybe." Sam gave Dev a pained look for his silence.

"Well, we'll all meet up at Domino's eventually and see if we can at least have a drink together."

"Definitely."

Doug stood and waved, "See you later."

"Bye!" When he left, Sam asked, "What's with you?"

"What did I do now?"

"You never said a word. Why did you join the club? You seem so dead set against socializing."

"I didn't want to ride all that way on my own."

"Why? Don't you have any friends?"

"What's that supposed to mean?" Dev took offense. "I've got friends, just none that want to ride to Sturgis. What's going on? Are you mad at me?"

"You just always seem on the edge of picking a fight."

"I am not!"

"Are too!"

Dev started laughing. "You mean like you are now?" Dev couldn't resist. He touched his fingertip to Sam's nose with a quick tap.

Predictably, Sam did a reconnaissance of the area.

"You're too irresistible." Dev rolled to his back, hands behind his head. "Tell me about your previous gay relationships."

"Why?" Sam faced him, lying on his side.

"I want to know how many times you've taken it up the ass."

"Enough."

"Like it?"

"Love it."

"Good."

"I'm not going to play the woman for you all the time. You have to reciprocate."

"Of course." Dev moved to mirror Sam's posture. "You are so handsome, Sam. I mean it."

"Thanks, Dev. The admiration is mutual."

"I'm hard."

"Surprise, surprise."

"I want to massage your balls again."

"Later."

Dropping to his back, Dev moaned in agony.

"You do it to yourself," Sam admonished.

"I do it to myself too much. That's the problem."

"That's not what I meant."

"I knew what you meant." Dev winked at him. Closing his eyes, he felt like drifting off to sleep, only he wanted to rest his head on Sam's chest when he did.

chapter Six

At seven the men walked to the Domino's Pizza booth. Members of their club were already waiting, chatting, laughing and all wearing the same T-shirts, except Tony who had on a black sleeveless tank exposing his tattoo and large deltoids.

Dev thought he would be a hunk if he wasn't such an ass.

"Hey, guys!" Sam greeted them cheerfully.

"Sam, Dev! How was your day?" Jerry asked.

"Good." Sam looked back at Dev.

Dev knew Sam was angry he was acting as both their mouthpieces again. But what was Dev supposed to add?

"We should order," Jerry advised. "Douglas, you got this whole table held?"

"Yeah, but I wouldn't mind someone else helping me out. In case someone gets funny."

"I'll do it," Sam offered.

"What do you want to eat?" Dev asked.

"Just two slices of pizza with mushrooms and onions, and a bottle of water."

When Dev held back his hand for cash, Sam said, "I was getting dinner, remember?"

Dev took his money, catching Tony watching them like a hawk.

Standing in the long, slow line, Dev finally got their order. The water bottles tucked under his arm, he carried two plates back and found Ralph, and Jerry and June had already joined Doug and Sam at the table.

"Here." Dev set Sam's plate in front of him, taking the space next to him. "Ice water for you, sir."

"Thanks."

"Your change." Dev held out his hand.

Sam cupped it and took back his cash.

"So? How do you like it so far, Devlin?" Jerry asked, munching on his pizza.

"It's okay." Dev chewed on his slice. "I've been here before. Though, I have to say, it's changed in fourteen years." He laughed, opening the plastic top to his bottled water.

"How old were you the last time?" Doug asked.

"Sixteen. But the first time I came with my mom and dad I was thirteen."

"That seems too young to be here," June added. "There's too much nudity."

"I suppose my father thought it was my rite of passage into manhood."

As Tony sat down he mocked, "When did you go off track?"

"Shut up," Sam whispered.

"What's all this?" Jerry asked, obviously ignorant to any strife.

"Never mind, Jerry." Sam continued as peacemaker.

Dev and Tony locked glares. Dev so much wanted to expose him for what he was, an ignorant homophobe.

"I wouldn't bring my kids here, period." Ralph gnawed at his pizza crust. "I think the amount of drugs and sex is too much of a bad influence."

"Then why are we here?" Doug found it very funny.

"For the bikes." Jerry waved around. "And the excitement."

"I don't think I'll come again," Ralph said. "Kay really gave me a hard time to be gone for this long. The kids are a handful sometimes."

"My wife didn't mind." Doug sipped his soda. "I think she was glad to get rid of me for the week."

"Yours too, Tony?" Dev teased. An elbow nudge to the ribs from Sam followed immediately.

"Least I got a wife. Not a boyfriend."

"Dev has an ex-wife," Sam corrected.

"Yeah, and now we all know why she's an ex."

Dev took a look around the table. Everyone was staring at him. "What?" He dared someone to ask him outright. He certainly wasn't ashamed and wouldn't lie.

"Anyway!" Sam obviously wanted the subject changed. "So, what's the entertainment tonight?"

"I'm sure they'll be a rock concert at the stage," Jerry replied.

"Yeah, but who the hell is Finger Eleven?" Ralph asked.

"No clue," Doug answered. "I'd rather just get drunk and watch all the lewd contests."

"That was my plan." Tony sipped his drink. "Sorry, Dev, it's chicks. Nothing you'd be interested in."

Jerry asked finally, "What's going on between you two?"

Dev caught Sam's silent plea and replied, "Nothing you need to worry about, Jerry." He finished his food.

"You should be asking that question of the two of them, not me." Tony pointed at Sam.

"I've had enough of your shit!" Dev growled, standing up and puffing out his chest.

"Come on!" Tony accepted the challenge.

"Sit down!" Sam grabbed Dev's shirt and dragged him to the seat.

"Look," Jerry leaned closer to them, "I don't want any of this shit from any of our boys, you got that?"

"Tell him that!" Dev snarled.

"Just quit the crap. I can't believe I'm having to act like a goddamn referee to two grown men! Grow the fuck up!" Jerry nudged his wife. "Come on, June. Let's get a beer." Before they left the table, June said sweetly, "You're all welcome to join us."

"Oh, thanks! Great." Sam pretended nothing was wrong.

Dev was about to kill someone.

As the rest of the gang stood one by one and dumped their trash, Dev felt his blood boiling. He and Sam were left on their own. "I do want to be a part of the group, Dev."

"That was the idea," Dev replied, "But just exactly how much am I supposed to take?"

"The highroad, Devlin. Take the damn highroad." Sam rose up and waited for him.

Exhaling a deep blast of air, Dev tossed out his meal debris and followed behind Sam and the rest to the nearest bar.

~

It was as packed as every other venue around the overcrowded campground.

Jerry had managed to get them a rectangular shaped table and they pulled as many spare chairs as they could find around it. A DJ was playing loud raucous music, interspersed with his running commentary about the upcoming events and his own dimwitted personal opinions.

Sam sipped his beer while Dev gulped his, seemingly intent on getting drunk.

"Slow down."

"Why? I'm here to party. If I had a joint I'd smoke it."

"Oh? Into drugs?" Sam asked.

"I am tonight."

"Stop sulking." Sam watched as Dev's angry eyes found Tony who had hooked up with two biker babes in halter tops.

"If I had my camera on me, I'd blackmail his ass."

"Dev, let's forget about him and enjoy ourselves."

"Yeah?" Dev faced Sam. "Going to kiss me?"

"Later."

"Whoopee."

"You don't want me to?" Sam peeked around quickly but the music was so loud he doubted anyone could be heard unless they were shouting.

"I want you to now."

"Dev, this is why I don't want you to get drunk."

"Stop being my mother, or my higher power, or god, or whatever the hell you are. I'm at a biker's fucking rally near Sturgis, and this is where mother-fuckers come to party. Look around."

Sam did. Many straight couples were groping and kissing. All drunk. And he smelled pot. It was lurking somewhere, but well hidden. The DJ ended a loud nail-scratching-on-blackboard tune, and announced a contest. As Sam watched in horror, unpleasant, tipsy looking females lined up. Hearing the details of the event, Sam cringed in revulsion.

Jerry, Ralph, and Douglas laughed heartily as June blushed brightly.

"You have to be kidding me." Sam winced.

"Isn't this nice?" Dev's voice was tinged with sarcasm.

As Sam gazed on in distaste, homely women sucked on large dick-sized pickles to see who could give them the best head.

"I'm gonna puke," Sam muttered.

The cheering from the crowd was intense. About to ask Dev to leave with him, he was let down when Dev ordered another beer. "You can't be serious about staying."

"What the fuck else is there to do? Go see some stupid heavy metal band I never heard of in a field with a hundred thousand drunk and stoned morons? Or better yet, you probably want to sit and talk at our tents, right, Sam? Talk but don't touch?"

"That's unfair." Sam grew enraged. "We did touch. We just did it discreetly."

Pointing back at the stage and the grotesque display, Dev replied, "Like that?"

Sam was loath to look. A large scantily dressed, tattoo-covered biker chick had an enormous dildo-pickle in her mouth. Sam flinched in disgust. As he turned away he caught Tony staring at him. A shiver of fear washed over him. "Christ, I'm in hell."

"What?" Dev asked.

"I said I'm in hell!" Sam shouted, immediately biting his lip after and peering around.

Dev shot his entire fresh beer down in one gulp, grabbed Sam's arm and said, "Let's go."

Doug asked, "You guys leaving?"

"Yeah, this isn't exactly our definition of entertainment," Dev replied.

"Really? If you wait, bet they start taking their shirts off."

Giving the stage another look, Sam couldn't help but recoil in disgust. "No thanks."

"I agree, they're not real beauties. That comes later on before the concert. Miss Buffalo Chip."

"Right." Sam tried to act enthused. "See ya."

They had to walk past Tony to the exit. Sam dreaded a confrontation.

He couldn't hear the words, but Tony had shouted something to Dev. "Oh, no." Sam watched Dev pause, yelling back. Closing in on them, Sam heard the battle commence.

"What's the matter, homo-boy? Can't stand a little chick action?"

"What I can't stand is the sight of you!"

Tony leaned closer to one of the girls he was holding and said very loudly, "He's queer!"

"And he's married!" Dev pointed back.

"So? Think she gives a shit? At least she's going to be with a real man!"

"You fucking prick!"

Sam grabbed Dev as he attempted to choke Tony. Several large bouncer-types quickly intervened.

"Out! Both of you!"

"Me?" Tony appeared shocked. "I was just standing here minding my own business when that fag attacked me."

Sam watched it register on the bouncer's face. "Out."

"Oh? Now he doesn't have to leave because he acts straight?" Dev countered.

"I said out!" The bouncer shoved Dev.

"Get lost, faggot!" Tony yelled, laughing.

"I don't believe this!" Dev tried to stand his ground.

Sam was going crazy watching the madness.

"Out. Go." The bouncer gripped Dev's arm.

"Get the fuck off me!" Dev brushed away the man's hand.

"Dev. Come on." Sam tried to intervene.

"Look, asshole," the bouncer shouted, "you want to be banned from the campsite?"

"For being a suspected homosexual? What the hell century is this?"

"Dev!" Sam grabbed Dev's elbow and dragged him outside the bar. Everyone in their immediate area was staring at them.

Hearing Tony's loud mocking, "Goodbye, queer-bait!" as they left, Sam felt Dev's body tighten in rage.

"Ignore him!" Sam begged. "You want to be thrown out?"

"Thrown out?" Dev dug in his heels outside the bar area. "Thrown out because I'm gay?"

"Shh!" Sam hated all the eyes on them.

"They can't do that! It's against the fucking law!"

"Dev, calm down!"

"I will not calm down! I have fucking rights!"

A passerby goaded, "Shut up, fag!"

Dev tore out of Sam's grasp and began pummeling the offender.

"Oh, shit!" Sam dove between them as did several other bystanders.

"Who you callin' a fag?" Dev punched the kid in the face again, a red river flowed down his knuckles from the kid's bloody nose.

Sam wrapped around Dev from behind, physically picked him up off his feet and carried him away before the wounded man decided to come back with either the cops or his mob of biker friends. "Let's go!"

Dragging Dev inch by inch, Sam looked back as Dev glared at every human being behind him. "Go. Now." Sam began pushing Dev, trying to get him back to their tents.

Loud amplified noise blew in the breezy air. The concert was about to begin with the Miss Buffalo pageant first. Sam could hear the roar of the crowds from where they were, almost a mile away. Finally coming closer to the camping area, the crowd thinned considerably. Dev jerked his arm away from Sam's grasp, heading to the men's toilet. Sam followed him in.

As Dev leaned over the sink to check his face, Sam asked, "Did he get you?"

"Yeah." Dev touched his cheek lightly.

"Wash the blood off your hand."

Dev looked down at it, sticking it under the running water. When he was done, he moved to a urinal and took a piss.

Sam watched in frustration. "Feel better? Had your battle?"

After he zipped up, Dev drew closer, threatening. "It's better than being stuffed back into the closet, chicken shit."

"I don't want a fight." Sam choked at the absurdity.

"Why not? Men fight for what they believe in. Ask your brother."

"Oh, that's a low blow. Especially coming from someone I considered a friend."

As if something broke in Dev, his rage vanished. "Fuck. I'm sorry."

"You should be. I came here to have a good time. Not to defend my honor or my brother's. I just wanted a light, happy party, Dev. I don't need to prove anything to anyone."

Wringing his hands, Dev looked like he was about to cry. "Don't you see? I can't help but defend myself, Sam. I'm not ashamed."

Sam looked around. They weren't alone. "You finished?"

"Let me wash my hands. You have to pee?"

"May as well while I'm here." Sam walked to the urinal. Once Sam unzipped his pants he found Dev trying not to be obvious as he stared. Shaking his head at him in admonishment, Sam relieved himself and wished he and Dev had met at another time. This wasn't what he had in mind for his first Sturgis rally, keeping a righteously proud gay man from getting clobbered or arrested.

It was nearing eight thirty and still showed no sign of getting dark. A strong wind whipped across the flat campgrounds and the tents were flapping and papers were blowing.

Following Dev to their site, they dropped down on their usual spots on the grass next to their bikes and relaxed.

"You really are a handful."

"And you're a chicken shit."

"Nice. Thanks." Sam snorted in annoyance. After looking around at the deserted area, since everyone was at an event, Sam peered down at Dev and found him touching his cheek. "Look at you, sore balls, sore face…"

"I wish I had a sore asshole."

That finally broke Sam's dour mood. He laughed and gazed at Dev in amazement. "I could really like you, Devlin, if you weren't so much goddamn trouble."

Dev rolled over to face Sam. "You realize no one is here."

Sam did.

"Wanna mess around?"

Standing, Sam took a good scan of the place to make sure not one human being was nearby. He realized they were completely alone except for a few senior citizens yards away sipping drinks at their canopy and tent. Sam bit his lip in uncertainty.

As if making a command decision, Dev crawled to his tent, opening it and getting inside.

Sam took another inspection of the area. No one was around. There were so many events it didn't make sense to sit in your tent. "What the hell." Trying to get inside quickly, Sam dove in and zipped up the tent behind him.

"Ouch."

"Sorry." He moved off of Dev's lower half, which he had landed on in his haste.

"Add sore shins."

"Aw, poor thing." Sam pouted his bottom lip and rubbed Dev's legs.

Instantly Dev sat up, cupped the back of Sam's head and drew him to his mouth.

Fire. Scorching, passionate fire. Sam moaned softly as Dev's tongue spun circles around his own. Coaxed downwards, Sam rested on top of Dev, feeling the large bulge of Dev's cock under his own. Sam went into a tailspin. He was so attracted to Dev physically all he wanted to do was be naked and rub against him. But he also knew, they had time after this crazy event to do it later on.

Inhaling Dev's scent, Sam felt his cock stand at attention. The man smelled so damn good. And his mouth? It was heaven. The way Dev kissed him, the passion, the adoration, he was soaking it up like pure honey. Dev's powerfully built body and masculinity were driving Sam wild.

Pulling up Dev's shirt, Sam touched the silkiness of the skin on Dev's sides. Meanwhile Dev had both his hands digging inside the back of Sam's jeans, cupping his ass cheeks. It was so hot, so erotic, Sam felt himself on the edge of orgasm already and dying for release.

With his left palm, Sam cupped Dev's face, feeling the scratchy shadow on his unshaven jaw. His right hand smoothed up Dev's chest to toy with his nipple. Under him Dev was humping like mad, pushing Sam against him as he did.

Pausing to stare at Dev's expression of intense longing, Sam teased his lips with the tip of his tongue, savoring the craving that was like pain on Dev's face.

"Christ, just fuck me, will you?" Dev moaned.

"Where's that condom?"

Stretching his neck to look, Dev found it on the tent floor.

"Lube?"

"Shit." Dev read the plastic wrapper. "It has some lube on it."

"That won't be enough."

"I don't care." Dev began taking off his shoes and socks.

"Dev, come on. I don't want to get your damn asshole sore as well."

"I said I don't care."

Sam leaned back as Dev stripped, kicking his clothing into the corner with his helmet and all the other items he had removed from his saddlebags.

"I do." Sam's cock throbbed at the sight of Dev naked.

"Be quiet," Dev scolded, kissing Sam again, yanking up Sam's T-shirt.

Breaking their kiss, Sam stared at Dev's body as he undressed. "You have any idea how much you turn me on?"

Dev smiled, rubbing Sam's hard-on through his jeans. "Yes."

Sam pushed his shoes and socks into a corner with Dev's and shimmied out of his pants.

"Christ! No underwear again?" Dev pumped his own cock at the excitement.

"Makes me feel sexy." Sam knew it would turn Dev on, and loved it!

"You are, make no mistake."

Sam rolled the condom on his penis, trying not to wipe off the lube it provided.

Dev spun over eagerly, getting to his hands and knees.

Moving behind him, Sam pressed the head of his cock against him. The tip slid in easily with the condom's lubrication.

"Push!"

"Hush! Don't talk so loud." Sam gently made his way in, feeling his body quiver at their first real union. He considered this the ultimate act, not the blowjob, and couldn't wait to enter Dev this way. He only wished it had been somewhere they could go wild and not in a cramped tent that you could hear a whisper through. "You okay?"

"Perfect."

Gliding in and out slowly, feeling the desire to own Dev, claim him, and screw his damn brains out, Sam assumed the lube wouldn't last and the friction would begin to make Dev raw. Resting over Dev's back, Sam stroked Dev's cock, knowing it would please them both and make him come faster. Just the touch of Dev's hot hard dick in his palm made Sam thrust his hips deeper.

"Sam... It feels amazing."

"No kidding..." Sam closed his eyes and pushed in until his balls were wedged against Dev's bottom. The penetration, this connection to Dev was so powerful, Sam felt the water sting his eyes from his desire. "Devlin. You feel so right."

Soon he was lost on the sensation, thrusting his hips and fisting Dev's cock. At a fast movement under him, Sam perked up, trying not to get too distracted. "You okay?"

"Just getting my towel so I don't get spunk on my bag, sorry."

"No. It's okay. I just want to make sure I'm not hurting you."

"You kidding me? I'm in heaven."

Smiling, Sam closed his eyes again and resumed his rhythm. Tingles raced over Sam's skin, and his balls tightened up as Dev's breathing quickened and his soft sounds of pleasure filled his ears. Dev's cock thrust into Sam's palm in an almost convulsive action. Instinctively squeezing it tighter and pushing his hips closer to Dev, Sam felt Dev's cock throbbing like mad.

Hearing Dev's grunting, feeling the hot sticky come on his hand, Sam came simultaneously, pressing his hips closer to Dev's ass to feel complete penetration.

"That's it, baby, shudder against me...oh, yeah."

Pausing until it subsided, Sam released his hold on Dev's cock and pulled out. "You okay?" Sam was so sated physically, he wanted to drop down and sleep with Dev cuddled against his chest.

"Yes. No problem." Dev removed the dirty towel from under him and rested on his back. "What are you going to do with that?" He pointed to the spent condom.

"No clue." Sam worked it off and held it by the top. "Any suggestions?"

"No." Dev laughed.

Sam carefully set it on top of Dev's towel and wedged it into the side of the tent where he wouldn't land on it.

"Come here."

Resting beside him, Sam smiled. "That was fantastic. I loved being inside you."

"I know. See why I couldn't wait?"

"Yes, but it'll still be better in one of our beds."

"I'm not so sure. I like the daring deed."

"That makes one of us." Sam listened for any suspicious noise around them.

"Shut up and kiss me." Dev closed his eyes.

Sam wrapped around him and sealed his body against Dev's. Since they were sexually satisfied for the time being, the kissing was leisurely and calm. Sam knew damn well he was falling for Dev. What more could he want? Looks, body, personality, talent? And a fantastic roll in the sack. Dev checked all the boxes as far as Sam was concerned, but he knew better than to have expectations.

Taking turns licking and teasing each other's tongues, Sam smiled in adoration. "You're a good kisser."

"So are you. And one hell of a lover."

"I haven't done anything yet. Not really."

"You sucked my dick and screwed me. Nothing? Not really?"

"I mean, not what we could do if we had the space, privacy, and time."

Dev ran kisses down Sam's neck and shoulder.

"When do you think everyone will start heading back?"

"I don't know. Midnight, one?"

Sam checked his watch. It was nearing nine. "You think so? Even Jerry and June? That seems a little late."

Dev kissed his neck. "What do you care?"

"Come on, Dev."

A look of complete exasperation appeared on Dev's face. "Not again!"

"I can't fall asleep here and wake up with you in the morning." Sam didn't understand why Dev couldn't see his point.

Flopping back to the tent floor, Dev rubbed his eyes in agony.

"Come on, Dev. Let's not fight over this." Sam ran his fingers over Dev's chest hair wishing he could be himself, knowing he couldn't.

"I can't keep arguing with you. You're draining the crap out of me with this constant paranoia."

Touching Dev's sore cheek, making him flinch, Sam asked, "This punch to the face wasn't enough?"

"I bet he got a broken nose."

"And you're proud of that?"

"I'm proud to mar any homophobe in punching distance."

"Don't start."

"You started it."

"Did not!"

"Did too!" Dev wrestled him, pinning Sam to the ground.

Laughing, Sam replied, "Did not."

Crushing Sam under him, Dev found his lips again for more kisses.

Oh, screw it. We have a few hours. Sam wriggled in excitement under him, wrapping around Dev and kissing back.

Chapter Seven

Sam opened his eyes. It was light out. Checking his watch, he found the time. It was seven in the morning.

A hot male body overlapped his, dewy sweat between them. Listening, Sam could hear voices of the campers around them. His heart began racing with anxiety. Tilting his head up, seeing their clothing scattered around in disarray, the towel with the spent condom on it in the corner, Dev's helmet...it appeared as chaotic and out of control as Sam's nerves. *Oh God no.*

Dev's arm rested over his chest. It rose and fell with Sam's rapidly increasing respirations of panic. Then to Sam's complete horror, Jerry's voice called out, "Dev?"

Shit! Sam kept stone still.

"Devlin? Sam?"

Sam wondered if Jerry could tell they were in the same damn tent.

"Are they there?"

"I don't know, June. Either they're asleep or they're already off somewhere."

"You want to come back after breakfast?"

105

"Well, that's just it. I don't want them to miss the pancakes."

Sam held his breath as June's shadow loomed closer.

"Devlin?"

Dev woke. "What?" he asked appearing very groggy.

Sam shook his head, holding his finger to his mouth.

"It's June and Jerry, Devlin. We just wanted to make sure you and Sam didn't miss the pancake breakfast."

Moving his limbs slowly, Dev replied, "Oh. Okay."

A second later Sam could hear June at his tent. "Sam?"

A bead of sweat rolled down Sam's temple.

"Sam? Are you in there?"

When Dev sat up and rubbed his face, Sam gripped his arm and made him meet his eye. "Don't say anything," Sam whispered.

June's voice was outside Dev's tent again. "Do you know where Sam is, Dev?"

"Probably the showers."

"Oh. Yes. Most likely. Well, when you find him, tell him we'll meet you two at the pancake breakfast."

"Okay."

"See ya, Dev," Jerry's voice began to recede as they walked away.

Finally moving from his frozen panic-stricken position, Sam sat up and caught Dev's scowl. Returning it, Sam knew this would cause an argument and hissed, "Don't start!"

Finding his jeans and T-shirt, Sam got dressed in the tight space as Dev kept up his glaring.

"Are you coming with me to wash up?"

His lip snarled, Dev replied, "You sure you want to be seen with a faggot?"

"Shut the fuck up. Let me get my shit together and we'll go."

Dev held out the used condom in annoyance, "Take this. It's yours."

In anger, Sam snatched it out of Dev's hand and climbed out of his tent. Why did Dev have to make it so difficult? It was driving Sam crazy.

Standing, looking at the many people passing by, Sam felt his skin crawl with the possibility someone would know they slept together and then the real trouble would begin.

~

Looking for a clean pair of briefs and his jeans, Dev found a black sleeveless T-shirt and tried to fold the rest of his clothing so it wasn't too much of a disaster inside his tiny tent. He was so upset with Sam's attitude, his face had a permanent frown. It was maddening since the sex was so damn good. Last night? Again, fantastic love-making, and what did they wake up to? A spat. Why couldn't Sam see that they should just behave as they liked? Everyone else was. Why couldn't they?

Gathering his towel and shaving kit, when he climbed out of the tent, Sam was waiting.

Without a word they walked to the bathrooms. Men were busy showering, shaving, talking loudly in the echoing room. After he brushed his teeth, Dev waited for a shower to become available, trying not to stare at Sam as he shaved at one of the sinks, remembering his big dick inside him and the taste of his kiss.

Getting his turn in the shower, Dev stripped and stood under the hot water, washing himself and feeling refreshed, even though he still brooded. It didn't seem fair that he and Sam couldn't play together, flirt, exchange sexy banter, nothing.

Once he shut off the taps, he grabbed his towel and noticed his come spattering it. Biting his lip from the intensity of the memory of Sam humping his ass and jerking him off, Dev fought with the same arguments he had in his head, over and over. He wanted to be out goddamn it! He was out! *Not this! Not back in the fucking closet!*

Using the shower head to rinse it off, Dev tried not to soak the whole towel since he needed it to dry himself. Avoiding the wet spot, Dev rubbed the towel over his hair and after wrapping it around his waist he stepped out so the next man could use the facility. He almost bumped straight into Tony.

At being caught unaware, something happened to both their expressions. Before Dev realized who it was, he admired the man's incredible body and knew he wasn't mistaken when he sensed the admiration coming back at him. It wasn't until their eyes met that the recognition of mortal enemies returned. And that slight attraction between them completely took Dev off guard.

Instantly their snarls of contempt returned.

Dev gave Tony a wide berth to avoid anymore contact. Besides, he wasn't about to fight with him naked and in front of a crowd of men.

With their eyes locked in a mental battle, Tony closed himself into the shower.

The reaction knocked Dev sideways. Standing still to regain his composure, Dev moved to a bench by the wall, finishing drying and dressing. Once he had his clothing on, he claimed a sink and shaved, his mind still assessing that odd incident and the implications that made no sense. But with a completely different interpretation it made all the sense in the world.

~

Sam had finished showering and dressing. He packed his toiletries away and draped his towel over his shoulder. Looking around the room he found Dev rinsing his face at the sink.

Instantly his heart melted from the sight. Dev was so damn attractive Sam had a hard time staying mad.

"Hey."

Dev dried his jaw and met Sam's eyes in the mirror. "Hey."

"Ready for pancakes?"

"Yup." Dev dropped his razor and shaving foam back into his small wash bag and carried it and his towel out of the building.

"You still upset with me?" Sam asked as he tossed his items into the tent, zipping it up.

"Huh?"

Standing tall, Sam tilted his head curiously. "You okay?"

"Yeah. Fine."

Having no idea why Dev was so distracted, figuring it had to do with their earlier argument, they headed to the free church breakfast in silence.

~

After their meal with Jerry, June, Doug, and Ralph, Sam and Dev returned to their tents.

"You're really quiet, Dev. What's going on?"

"Hm?" Dev looked back at him, preoccupied. "Quiet?"

"Yes. You're in a dream world."

"Am I?" Dev retrieved his leathers from the saddlebag.

"Yes."

"Just tired." Dev threw the leather clothing inside his tent so he could change into them.

"So? First Mount Rushmore, then up to Sturgis?" Sam asked.

"That's the plan."

"Good."

Dev climbed into his tent, stripping off his jeans and tugging on his leather pants. He knew he must be mistaken. That look from Tony wasn't attraction or admiration. No doubt Tony was reminiscing about his romp in bed with some biker chick. That had to be it.

~

Though his butt was still slightly worn out, Dev rode along side Sam southbound on the picturesque winding Highway 16. Hundreds of Harleys were on the same road, and cruising with a pack of so many strong was invigorating. Tractor trailer trucks blasted their horns in greeting, locals in pickup trucks waved and cheered. It was a welcoming party of the grandest scale. Dev's mood elevated once again for the reason he had come. Solidarity.

Having been to Mount Rushmore previously, Dev wondered what Sam's feedback would be. It was an amazing sight.

As they wound into the park limits, Dev slowed down knowing the carved mountain would be coming into view shortly and he wanted to witness Sam's reaction to it.

The minute they could see the exposed face, Dev received Sam's enthusiastic thumbs up.

Finding the parking lot crammed with bikes, Dev stopped and shut down the engine, flipping up his face shield.

"Holy shit!" Sam gasped, his eyes never leaving the enormous carving on the mountainside.

"Impressive, isn't it?" Dev grinned broadly.

Dismounting the bike, Sam headed closer, drawn like a moth to fire.

Dev took his digital camera with him, hurrying behind Sam to walk to the viewing area together.

In the heat and brilliant sunshine, they stood with a hundred riders and tourists to gape in disbelief.

"I can't get over how big it is," Sam gushed. "I really didn't expect that."

"It is unbelievable. I remember the first time I saw it as a kid." Dev stepped back and took a shot of Sam with the mountain behind him. He tapped a young woman's arm. "Could you take a photo of me and my friend?"

"Sure!"

Dev handed her the camera, moved to Sam and put his arm around his waist. Half expecting Sam to shove him off, he was pleasantly surprised to feel his arm wrap around his back. They smiled and the young lady took the shot. When she handed it back to Dev he thanked her, quickly checking the tiny monitor to see it.

Sam stood next to him. "You handsome devil."

"Me?" Dev laughed at the absurdity.

"Can you get closer to it?" Sam pointed.

"No. This is it." Dev took another photo.

Taking a moment to allow Sam to gaze at the monument in silence, Dev turned back to look at the parking lot and its collection of motorcycles, campervans, trucks, and cars. A group of men in denim vests and black leather pants were walking their way up to the viewing area. Several of the men were holding hands.

Dev choked in astonishment and nudged Sam.

"What?"

"Look at that."

Sam twisted to where Dev was staring. "Are you kidding me?"

As the group of men approached, Dev quickly made his way to one of the couples. Boldly touching the man's arm and turning him around to read the club's name on the back of his denim vest, Dev gasped, "A gay club? Here?"

"You got a problem with that?" The big man with a shaved head and full mustache puffed up in fury.

"No! I'm so happy to see you guys I could kiss you!"

"Come to papa." The man held out his arms.

"Well, I was only kidding." Dev blushed, looked over his shoulder at an astonished Sam and said, "What the hell." Dev hugged him and pecked his lips.

"Where are you from?" one of the other men asked.

"Dayton."

"Are you with a gay club?"

"No. Unfortunately not, and to be honest, I've already run into some problems."

"You should hang with us." A very macho looking black man with tattoos and a bandana on his head stepped closer.

"I should." Dev gazed back at Sam who had kept his distance.

"You missed the gay biker's run. It was yesterday."

"Damn! I just got here. But I wasn't really up to an extra ride." Dev looked back at Sam and in exasperation he waved him over.

"Is that your partner?"

"Yes. Christ, he's become so paranoid he's driving me nuts."

"What's his name?"

"Sam."

"Sam!" the shaved headed biker yelled. "Get your tight butt over here."

Sheepishly Sam obeyed.

The bold man gripped Sam's jaw and asked, "You don't be afraid of nothing or nobody. You got that?"

"Yeah? What fantasy world do you guys live in?" Sam shook his head at the absurdity.

"Ride with us."

"We have our own group," Sam explained.

"Fuck them."

"Yeah, fuck them," Dev echoed.

"Dev..." Sam chided. "We already have reservations at a campsite."

Throwing up his hands, Dev explained, "See what I'm up against?"

The bald biker grinned wickedly, "I wouldn't complain if I were up against him."

Groaning in delight, Dev announced, "This is what I love about being around gay men."

"Well, the invitation is standing, or lying, whichever you want." The man's eyes twinkled impishly. "Here. This is our pamphlet and where our booth is set up in Piedmont." He unfolded something from his back pocket.

Dev took the paperwork. "Thanks."

"Nice to meet you. Both of you. Good luck."

Dev shook the man's hand and watched them walk down the paved path.

When he spun around Sam had that look to him, the one that seemed to want to disassociate himself with all things gay. "You're pissing me off again."

"And I can't believe you kissed that guy in public. You have any idea how many people spied it?"

"I give up." Dev started heading to his bike, hearing Sam's footfalls right behind him.

"Let's ride through Sturgis. Grab a bite," Sam suggested, putting on his helmet.

"Whatever." Dev didn't know how much more of this closet attitude he was willing to take.

~

Trying to forget their difference of opinion and enjoy himself, as they made it finally to Sturgis, Sam was in awe. Yes, he knew half a million motorcycles would descend upon this tiny town, but seeing it was beyond his imagination.

Down the main street were four columns of bikes parked horizontally, and it seemed to go on and on for miles. A constant parade of tricked out choppers and semi-naked riders cruised proudly like an ad for Harley Davidson or a film trailer for *Easy Rider*. Sam didn't know which. With Dev cruising along at a slow pace in front of him, Sam gazed in astonishment at the men and women who were looking back at him and his friend. Kawasakis weren't the norm, so they caught many eyes. As if Dev had a destination in mind, Sam followed him off the main drag to a parking lot full up with more bikes. Sam figured every motorcycle rider in America had shown up. The amount of metal and chrome was making him dizzy.

Stopping, shutting off the engine, Sam removed his helmet from his sweating head and read a sign over the entrance of the building. Full Throttle Saloon. It appeared to be the type of place you'd see in a Western and he anticipated a shootout and someone to come flying out of the front doors. Unzipping his jacket in the heat, he followed Dev inside.

Instantly hit with the aroma of cigarettes, pot, booze, and sweat, Sam gaped in shock as he took it in. Some women inside cages were topless and large, rough boys were gawking at them from outside.

"Oh, no way." Sam touched Dev's arm. "Not here. Isn't there a café close by?"

"I want a beer."

"Beer? You'll be riding back."

Dev tugged out of Sam's hold and walked up to the counter. Sam grimaced at Dev's "attitude", which Sam had hoped would lighten up. Obviously it hadn't. He knew Dev was still brooding over the comments made earlier.

In the mob at the bar, one lone bar stool was unoccupied. Dev removed his leather jacket and tossed it over the top. "What have ya got on tap?" Dev shouted to the bartender.

Taking off his own jacket, Sam rested it over of Dev's and with two fingers, pinched his wet t-shirt off his skin, fanning it, to try and cool off, which wasn't likely in the stuffy room. Women *and men* walked by in black riding chaps with their thong-covered ass cheeks hanging out.

The sight of the men exposing themselves in that way in such a macho environment completely confused Sam.

Dev handed him a frosty beer mug. About to refuse it to avoid drinking and riding, Sam caught several hardy individuals studying him. He was glad he wasn't wearing his "possibly gay looking" club T-shirt. Suddenly he imagined it would be like a red cape to a bull. He took the damn beer.

Sipping the refreshing ale, Sam almost choked as Dev stripped off his shirt and used it to wipe his face. None of the men in the room were shirtless. Several had denim or leather vests over bare skin, showing off their tattoos; which on many appeared to be blue sleeves. The sight of Dev's fantastic ripped chest and abs naked over his black leather jeans was something Sam expected at a gay bar, not a biker bar. Instantly he was nervous that someone would think that they were gay, and the trouble would begin. They were so outnumbered, it would be a slaughter.

As Dev casually leaned back against the bar next to him, Sam watched all the action around them, and there was plenty to see. The most bizarre was a cage and pit where men would attempt to burn out their motorcycle tires in a tar-stinking-squealing hole of hell while topless women assisted.

"Hey." A scantily leather-clad blonde bombshell made her way towards Dev.

Sam bristled but kept his mouth closed.

"Hey." Dev smiled.

The woman boldly used her index finger to smooth down the center of Dev's chest to the top of his leather pants. "Nice."

"Thank you," Dev replied, his eyes flickering to Sam's as he watched.

When the woman brashly licked Dev's pectoral muscle and gave Dev a seductive, inviting grin, Sam was about to combust. "Dev," he tried to keep from screaming at him. "You ready to go?"

"No." Dev gave his attention back to the sultry blonde.

Sam's blood began to boil. He knew exactly what this was all about. And it was infuriating him.

In the balmy room where there seemed to be no rules or reason, Sam witnessed the blonde cupping both her hands over Dev's chest muscles. He couldn't take another minute. "Dev!"

"What?" Dev replied in the same exasperated tone.

"Let's go."

"What's his problem?" the woman sneered.

"Why don't you ask him?" Dev replied, taking another casual sip of beer.

Either Sam was going to shove that woman off his man and get clobbered by all those who were watching, or he needed to storm out. After slamming his empty beer mug on the counter, Sam grabbed his jacket and helmet and left in a huff.

Outside in the broiling sun, Sam stood still ready to scream in frustration. The amount of pain Sam was feeling at the sorry little show of Dev's upset him terribly. Sam had been burned before. He knew better than to feel infatuation for someone so quickly.

Moving away from the entrance, standing near his bike, he imagined taking off without Dev, back to the campsite, to Spearfish Canyon, to the Needles, anywhere but having to witness a woman pawing at his lover.

He ended up doing nothing except sitting on his bike in the baking heat, waiting. Torn between giving up on this budding relationship, and wanting Devlin so badly he ached, Sam was miserable.

What seemed like an eternity passed. Sam noticed Dev finally exiting the bar, his T-shirt back on his torso, his helmet in one hand, jacket in the other.

When they met up, Sam glared at him in hatred.

Dev met his stare and returned it. "What's wrong, Rhodes? I thought you wanted me to act straight? Am I wrong again?"

"I knew you were doing it to piss me off."

"Oh no!" Dev replied in pure sarcasm. "It was to please you. To pacify your closet tendencies I was willing to hide behind breasts for you, asshole!"

"Shut up! I hate you. You know that?"

"What do you want from me?" Dev roared.

People's heads turned at the growing volume but Sam forced himself not to look or be afraid.

"To just cool it. To act like a friend and let's just have a good time." Sam's heart was breaking.

"On your terms?"

"Forget it." Sam struggled to put his jacket on and didn't want to in the heat.

Dev gripped the leather of Sam's sleeve in his fist and dragged him closer. "You can't have it both ways," Dev hissed. "Make a fucking decision."

Sam shoved him off violently, unable to stop himself from scanning the area. Shaking as he put on his helmet, Sam wanted to go home. That was it. Who needs this crap?

Dev watched him, arms crossed over his large pecs. "Where're you going?"

"What the fuck do you care? Go screw your bimbo!"

"I don't want a woman. How many times do I have to tell you that?"

"Shut up." Sam felt his skin crawl as men stared at them as they strolled past.

In complete aggravation, Dev threw up his hands and walked away.

Sam's bottom lip trembled as Dev left. He didn't want Dev to go off without him. He wanted them to be together. Waiting to see if Dev would look back, change his mind, do something positive for them as a couple, Sam was disappointed. Dev vanished.

~

Head down, Dev dragged his leather jacket and helmet with him as he went, wishing he could throw them aside and feel unburdened. It was bad enough his heart was breaking, he didn't need the baggage, literally. Yes, he tormented Sam on purpose. To make a damn point. If Sam was intent on them hiding behind a mask of heterosexual behavior, fine! Dev knew what he was doing, taunting Sam. But he had hoped it would prove to Sam that they didn't need to pretend. Unfortunately his plan didn't work. Obviously he didn't know Sam well enough to predict his reaction.

Seeing a shady bench in front of a store, Dev dropped down, slapping his gear next to him, and covered his face in anguish. Inhaling to calm himself down, he removed his mobile phone from his pocket and dialed home. He had to talk to someone or he would burst.

"Hello?"

"Dad?"

"Hiya, Dev! Having fun?"

Waiting as a loud Harley drove by, Dev replied, "No."

"Oh?"

"Dad, that guy I met, Sam?"

"Uh oh. What?"

"He's driving me crazy."

"I take it, not in a good way?"

"No."

"Look, that's the breaks. You'll meet someone else."

"I don't want to meet someone else."

"You have it that bad for him? And you just met him?"

"Yes."

"Christ, Dev...if he doesn't want a relationship, screw it. Don't get yourself into an emotional state."

"No. It's not that. He does want me."

"Then what the hell's the problem?"

"He keeps wanting me to act straight while I'm here. I can't even touch him unless we're hiding in the tent at night."

"Devlin, listen to him. You know damn well I agree with him."

"Why?" Dev whined, glaring at two women whose stare lingered too long.

"Dev, you'll be out of there by Sunday. For Christ's sake, keep your mitts off him for a couple of days."

"I knew I'd get this from you. Put Mom on the phone."

"She's busy. You listen to me, Devlin. I've been to that rally before."

"Years ago! You know there's a gay biker group from Arizona here?"

"Dev..."

"Forget it, Dad."

"Dev!" his father shouted, "Don't do it! I'm telling you now, don't do it!"

"Whatever. Gotta go."

"Don't hang up!"

Dev disconnected him, shutting off the phone because he knew his dad would call back. Slipping it into his leather jacket pocket, Dev raised the bottom of his shirt to wipe the sweat off his face. He didn't want to hear he was wrong. He wanted someone to tell him to be proud of what he was, to stick to his guns, to show the world he was gay and not be ashamed. Why couldn't they see it his way?

~

Sam showed his ID wristband to the employee at the gate at the campground and was allowed access. Riding slowly through the congested area to the campsite, Sam was glad to see their little tents still standing unmolested and parked his bike in front. Shutting it down, he immediately entered his tent to strip off the leather and dress in a pair light shorts instead. Then, before he left the privacy of the enclosure, he paused, thinking about everything. Flopping back to rest on his sleeping bag, Sam wanted to talk to Dev, but it seemed inevitable they had to agree to disagree. He understood Dev's point. Knew it to death. But being open and out was for later. At home. And even in the sleepy suburb of Centerville, one had to use common sense. Ohio was almost a part of the Bible Belt and there were individuals who still believed what they did was a sin. But Sam didn't care about it back home. He was out there. He didn't need to hide who he was in Ohio and going about his day to day life. This was an exception.

Thinking about the type of men who were in that bar, wincing at seeing his beautiful man in the arms of a woman, Sam covered his face in anguish wishing Dev could just be patient, and see how good it could be next week, on his terms, where Sam felt more secure.

"Not here, Dev. Please. Not here."

~

By five Dev was beginning to get road weary. He'd toured the Black Hills and Spearfish Canyon, but hated to admit he didn't pay much attention to the fantastic scenery. He was so wrapped up with his internal dialogue he was in a daze. Arguing in his head about Sam, wondering if things would work between them since they were already fighting at such an early stage, Dev felt sick to his stomach about it.

Waiting in the long line to get back into the campgrounds, Dev showed his ID bracelet and was allowed in. When he pulled up to their tents, Sam's bike was there but Sam wasn't.

Shutting down the motor, climbing off and into his tent to shed the hot outfit, Dev was exhausted. He knew he needed to eat something since he'd had nothing but a beer since the pancake breakfast. Stripped down to just his gym shorts, he relaxed on the sleeping bag and closed his eyes to nap in the heat.

~

Waking, a pool of sweat on his face from where he had been lying on his forearm, Dev sat up and tried to clear his head. He had slept for almost two hours and the sensation of lethargy was frustrating.

Unzipping the tent, he staggered to the toilet to wash his face and wake up. At a sink, running the cold water and rinsing the sweat off his skin, Dev gazed in the mirror and was unhappy with his reflection. He looked miserable. Missing Sam more than he wanted to admit, he wondered where the hell he was in the chaos. *Baby, where are you?*

Returning to his tent, Dev changed into his jeans and his black sleeveless tee, sat down on the grass and dialed Sam's mobile phone number. The service picked up. Dev didn't leave a message. Lingering, hoping Sam would pop back, after a half hour Dev gave up. Moving their bikes together, Dev chained them up, hid his leathers in the saddlebags, and took a walk to get some food.

Standing on his own eating a bison burger and sipping a cola, Dev felt lonely and wondered if Sam had met up with Jerry and the rest of the group. After he'd finished his meal, he located the nearest bar and decided not to bother hunting anyone down. He'd see Sam later at the tent. Hopefully Sam wasn't too angry with him and they would talk then.

~

While the Miss Buffalo Chip pageant continued on a stage behind him, Sam drowned his sorrows on his fifth beer. "The boys" of the group were whistling and howling like animals at the display of babes in bikinis. Sam was so bored he could sleep where he sat.

Checking his watch, wondering where Dev was, Sam decided on finishing his beer and heading back to the tents to have a look for him. He missed him so badly he needed to see him again. Imaging the rest of the tour without him was making Sam feel ill.

"You going?" Ralph asked. "They haven't even chosen a winner yet."

"I'm beat. I need a walk to wake up. You can fill me in on what I missed later."

"Okay."

Sam avoided the odd stares from the men who thought there was no better entertainment in the state than what they were watching at the moment.

Making his way out of the Black Parrot bar, Sam felt jostled by the crowd and imagined Dev waiting eagerly for him at their cozy spot and catching up on what they had done separately. At least Sam hoped he'd be there and in an amiable mood. Remembering Dev carried his mobile phone, Sam checked his pockets and regretted leaving his in his bike's locked saddlebag. They had to work this out. Somehow come to a compromise. Sam felt he had already, meeting with Dev in the night, but obviously that wasn't enough for the bold and self-righteous Devlin Young.

~

"Another shot, and a beer chaser, please?" Dev asked the bartender. Drunk, pissed off, wishing Sam was with him, Dev thanked the bartender and handed him cash. Sniffing the strong whiskey, Dev tossed it down his throat and shivered at the potency. After setting down his shot glass, he gulped the cold beer to rid the foul aftertaste of the liquor.

"Buy a gal a drink, sailor?"

Dev moved his drunken gaze to a young woman in a Harley T-shirt standing next to him. "No thanks."

Though it seemed she was about to make a snide comment, he was surprised when instead she just walked away.

A moment later, a male voice whispered behind him, "Where's your boyfriend?"

Rubbing his face in agony, Dev moaned, "Leave me alone."

"He break up with you?" Tony teased.

"I said, leave me alone."

"Drowning your sorrows? Can't find someone else to suck your gay cock?"

Dev spun around and glared at him. "Go away!"

Making a clicking sound with his tongue, Tony pouted his lip out in exaggeration. "Poor fag, drinking all alone. The pariah of the group."

Stumbling off the bar stool, Dev grabbed Tony by his shirt. "Why are you always on me? Huh?"

Tony shrugged off Dev's grasp. "Don't touch me, faggot."

Dev shoved Tony back towards the exit. "What'd I ever do to you?"

"Watch it, Dev!" Tony snarled in warning.

"No! You watch it!" Dev forced him outside the bar and into a flow of pedestrians.

"Stop pushing me!" Tony shoved him back.

Regaining his balance Dev gripped Tony in a headlock and dragged him off the main drag behind the bar where the dumpsters and trashcans were hidden.

"Get off me!" Tony yelled, trying to escape the hold.

"I think I know what your fucking problem is, man." Dev trapped Tony with his body weight against the outer wall of the bar. "You're a closet gay. Am I right?"

That caused Tony to go berserk. Growling like a wildcat, Tony broke the grasp and grappled with Dev to get even. With Tony's strong grip on his shoulders, Dev was twisted around and his back slammed into the same wall. His breath hissed out of him from the impact.

"Asshole! I should kill you!" Tony roared.

Knowing Tony was full of crap and there was something else going on, Dev grabbed Tony's head and planted a kiss on his lips.

Jerking away from the contact, Tony's eyes were wild with fury. He spat on the ground and began swinging for Dev's face with wild roundhouse punches. Stumbling awkwardly, completely drunk, Dev ducked under a right hook, clamping onto Tony's neck and bringing him back to his mouth. The contact to Tony's lips, the bristles of his goatee, made Dev's cock go rock hard.

"Stop!" Tony snarled through clenched teeth. "You filthy faggot!"

"You know you want it. You son of a bitch! You don't think I can see right through you?" Dev clamped his hands around Tony's neck.

Tony's nails scratched Dev's arms as he struggled to get away. Dev wasn't about to let him. Tony kneed him in the groin, just missing a direct hit into Dev's balls. Pivoting his body to deflect the strike, feeling it crash into his hip painfully, Dev spun them around again until Tony's back was smashed against the wall. The impact caused the air to escape from Tony's lungs temporarily, making him vulnerable.

As Tony gulped for a breath, Dev cupped his hand over Tony's crotch and felt a large erection under his black jeans. "You stupid son of a bitch! Admit you love this!" Dev felt his heart pounding in excitement wanting to drag Tony's clothing off and suck his big cock.

Pressing Tony as hard as he could, pinning him to the wall with all his weight, Dev hissed sensuously, "You have the fucking nerve to taunt me? You know you want me to suck it."

"Get away from me," Tony whined, his expression overcome with anguish.

"Don't you ever taunt me again. You hear me, you bastard? You know damn well what's going on between us." Dev was gasping for breath and dripping in sweat from the warm air and battle. Reacting to what he imagined was going to be a punch to the face, Dev twisted back and was caught by Tony's hands. To his astonishment, Dev's jaw was forced to Tony's open lips.

Wildly excited after the violence, Dev writhed against Tony's hard body, drawing at this gorgeous fucker's mouth like a vacuum, he could barely hold back his excitement.

A sound of someone shouting alerted the men that they had been spied. "Hey! What the hell are you fags doing?"

"Oh, shit." Dev pulled apart from Tony quickly.

"No…" Tony moaned when he realized they had been seen.

Two tattoo-covered, muscle-bound men approached them menacingly.

Immediately Tony pointed at Dev. "He's queer and tried to rape me!"

"What?" Dev roared in betrayal, "You lying bastard!"

The men surrounded Dev, impelling him back against the wall.

"Tony!" Dev shouted. "Don't do this to me!"

"We don't like it when fags try to assault straight boys," one snarled through crooked teeth.

"Tony!" Dev tried to see over their shoulders but he couldn't tell if Tony had deserted him. "Look, he's lying!"

"We could see what was going on. You were the one attacking him." The second man's lip curled as he trapped Dev against the bricks with his palm on Dev's shoulder.

"Bullshit! I'm telling you he's lying. Why do you believe him and not me?"

"Cause you look like a fag, pretty boy."

"What the hell's that supposed to mean?" Dev tried to shove the man back but it was like moving cement. Dev felt his stomach tighten and the fear in him was like white fire, burning his skin.

"You wanted to rape him? What if we want to rape you?"

"Shit. Tony!" Dev tried to get away, the drops of sweat running off his forehead stinging his eyes. The anger in the men's eyes was terrifying. Dev knew he was dead.

"Not so fast, homo-boy."

"I'm telling you he's lying. I'm not gay!" As he said those words, all the warnings from his dad and Sam washed over him like a poltergeist. *They were right. God, they were so right.*

126

A powerful punch landed on Dev's jaw. Feeling he had everything to lose, he went crazy, like his father used to do. He forced one of the men back, using the brick wall for leverage, and swung at the second. Making contact on the man's face, Dev heard the impact and felt the pain in his knuckles from catching the man's teeth. Ducking down like a linebacker, Dev slammed his shoulder into the second man as he came at him, knocking him to the ground. Dev ran for the mainstream of pedestrians but felt one of the men on his back, their arm round his neck, choking him, dragging him backwards.

"Help! Someone!" Dev tried to pry the man's forearm loose from his throat.

A hand covered his mouth to stop his cries.

Dev bit it, causing it to jerk away. He stomped down on the man's foot and growled in fury as he twisted around to confront him. More punches were thrown, one split Dev's lip, several others pounded into his chest and stomach. Trying not to fall to the ground and become a kicking bag, Dev booted the man in the groin and he staggered back in pain. The second man was on him instantly. Dev heard his T-shirt rip as he wrenched to get free. As the man dragged him back, deeper into the isolated alley, Dev pushed the heel of his palm under the man's jaw, tilting his head backwards, forcing him away from him. The battle was exhausting him and being drunk wasn't helping. He didn't know how much more he could take. He was sapped of strength and wanted someone to come and help him.

In a brief pause in the struggle, Dev held out his hand, hoping they were as tired as he felt. "Leave me the fuck alone," Dev yelled. "You're both insane. I didn't do anything. Why are you doing this to me?"

It only seemed to infuriate them. With a man on either side of him, Dev was thrown face first into the wall. Tilting his head back so his jaw didn't get smacked, he felt one of them trying to open his jeans. "No! Get the fuck off me! Help! Someone, help! Oh God! No!"

~

Sam paced. He wanted Dev to show up. It was driving him crazy imagining Dev with a woman, or another man. They needed to talk this out. It couldn't be over before it started.

Checking his watch, he located his mobile phone and called Dev's number. The answering service picked up. "Where are you? I'm at the tent." Pausing, not knowing what else to say, wanting to add he missed him, Sam hung up. Dropping down to the grass as the sky grew pale, Sam waited. Getting emotional at being let down, yet again, Sam gazed at the two motorcycles, connected together by a chain. He wished from the time Dev finally showed up at the tent to meet him, he could chain Dev to himself as well. The amount he missed him was disconcerting. Did he really feel this strongly about Dev so early in their friendship? Though Sam wanted to deny it, he already knew the answer.

~

"Get off me! You have to be kidding me. What the hell do you think you're doing?" Dev growled as one of the men dragged his jeans down his thighs. "Help! Someone!" Dev imagined crying rape. Never in his life did he ever think he would be shouting out that word in a dark alley. This was insane!

Knowing this was going to get very ugly, very quickly if he didn't do something, Dev forced himself to find some inner reserve of energy and fight back.

As his pants were yanked down his ass, Dev went ballistic. "No!" Thrashing violently, Dev head-butted backwards and caught one of them in the face. He spun around when he could and discovered blood rushing from the man's nose. Just as Dev

128

was hiking up his clothing, the other one dove at Dev in retaliation. They head-locked like two wrestlers, ramming each other against the dirty bricks of the walls. Roaring in fury, Dev kneed him in the groin, as hard as he could, made a direct hit, and the man fell back against the dumpster and curled up in pain.

Trying to close his pants, facing the man with the bloody nose, Dev was rushed by him, even while the river of red gushed out of the man's nostrils.

Feeling the man trying to knee him in the nuts in retaliation for what Dev did to his buddy, Dev kept pivoting his hips to avoid a painful strike. Dev wanted to get this man off him while his friend still writhed on the ground. Going for a second butt in the head, Dev smashed into the man's bloody nose with his forehead and caused enough pain for the man to stagger back. Using the split second opportunity, Dev darted out of the alley.

~

Growing weary, Sam assumed Dev was busy for the night. Maybe he found one of those gay biker men and was off screwing. Seeing Tony trying to pass by unnoticed, Sam stood up and hurried to him. "Hey."

"What do you want?"

Stunned by the aggression, Sam threw up his hands. "Just wanted to know if you've seen Dev. Never mind!"

Tony looked back over his shoulder, glared at Sam in hatred and left.

Shivering at the "if looks could kill" gaze he'd endured from Tony, Sam was about to give up and head back to the events. Maybe he could find Ralph or Jerry to hang out with.

Before he could make his way through the crowd, Sam noticed Dev staggering towards him on the dusty road.

Racing for him, Sam held his arms and moaned, "Oh no. Oh, God, no." Wrapping around his waist, Sam helped Dev to the men's toilet and soaked paper towels to dab at his bloody eyebrow and lip. "Oh, shit. Dev, let me take you to a first aid station. You need a stitch in that eyebrow."

"No." Dev flinched from the pain of Sam's pressure on his cuts.

Once he had his face clean of all the blood, Sam instructed Dev, "Hold this wet compress on your cut to allow the bleeding to stop." While Dev held his forehead, Sam inspected Dev's body. His T-shirt was torn, his arms and back were scratched with red raised welts. Under his breath, Sam began crying, "I knew this would happen."

Dev wrapped around him, resting on him.

Holding Dev tight, feeling horrible for him, Sam realized people were looking, but he tried not to care. "Come on."

Sam led Dev out of the men's room and helped him crawl into his tent, following him in. After zipping up the flap for privacy, Sam helped Dev remove his damaged shirt. The scratches went down to the waistband of Dev's jeans. "What happened? Do I need to ask?"

Dev touched his bruises lightly, not answering.

"Let me get that first aid kit you said you brought."

Gingerly reaching into his front pocket, Dev handed Sam his keys. "Black box behind the seat."

"Okay. I'll be right back." Biting his lip to stop his tears, Sam trembled as he opened the shiny black container. This was exactly what he knew would happen if either of them came out in this place. He could have written the damn script.

A small red kit was inside. Sam opened it, found it was the correct one, and locked the case up again. When he crawled back into the tent, Dev was lying on his side.

Closing them in, Sam opened the little box and removed some antibiotic cream and adhesive strips. Gently urging Dev to his back, Sam attended his slit eyebrow and rubbed ointment on his cracked lip lightly. Using an alcohol wipe, Sam cleaned the dirt out of his scratches. "How come they go so far down your body, Dev?"

Dev didn't answer.

Sam reached to unbutton Dev's jeans to see for himself. Dev's hand grabbed Sam's quickly, stopping him.

Inhaling a sharp breath, Sam said, "I just want to help."

Releasing him again, Dev closed his eyes.

Sam opened his button and unzipped his jeans, loosening them so he could see down the back. The scratches seemed to keep going. Sam didn't even want to guess why they were so low down his hips. Using the medicated wipes to clean them the best he could, Sam forced himself to ask, "What happened, Dev? How did the scratches manage to get under your jeans?"

Dev's eyes met Sam's and the agony in them made his breath catch in his throat. "No. No, Dev, please tell me it's not what I am thinking."

"Almost. But no."

In agony, Sam wrapped around Dev, crying over his shoulder. "I'm sorry. I'm so sorry."

"What are you sorry about? You warned me."

"I should never have left you. I should have stayed with you." Sam felt so guilty he was dying inside.

"You're not my babysitter."

"No. But I'm your friend." Sam set back from Dev, wiping his tears with his shirt tail.

Dev closed his eyes.

Trying to offer comfort, Sam petted his hair softly, allowing him to rest, sick to his stomach at what Dev had suffered and how close he came to being raped.

131

chapter Eight

When Dev opened his eyes he was alone in his tent. Checking his watch, seeing it was almost eight, he touched his face hesitantly and flinched at the pain. Rolling over on his sleeping bag, Dev didn't want to see what he looked like. He could well imagine how beat up he was. He and Tony were well matched now. Two men with bruised faces.

That kiss. That haunting kiss.

Tony grabbing his jaw and...

"God. No way. Not that idiot." Dev moaned rubbing his temples as his head began to ache instantly remembering the betrayal. How could Tony do that to him? How could he set him up for an execution and leave? That horrible bastard!

Dev wanted to choke Tony he was so destroyed at the act of treachery. Dev knew if he wasn't as fit as he was he would have been a sitting duck. Tears welling in his eyes, stinging them, Dev felt so let down by Tony's behavior, he was beating himself up for it now as much as those two goons did in the alley. He was the sucker. He's the one who brought Tony to back of the building to kiss. This was his fault, not Tony's. Dev curled up in a ball and wept.

And Sam. Sam's steadfast friendship. How could he do what he did to Sam? Dev cried for himself, in self-pity and in anger, wishing he had listened to his father and his friend.

Dozing on and off from his exhaustion, Dev heard Sam's sweet voice calling. "Dev?"

"Yeah."

"You want to go get some breakfast?"

Dev didn't answer. He wanted to go home.

"Dev?"

When the front flap zipper opened and Sam poked his head in, Dev raised his head to see him.

"You feel okay?"

His reply dripping in sarcasm, Dev said, "I'm great. Never felt better." Regretting his tone soon after. He knew he was mad at himself and shouldn't be taking it out on Sam. But he couldn't help it. Wasn't this Sam's fault as well? If Sam would allow them to be a couple, Dev wouldn't have been on his own last night. Right?

Rolling his eyes at him, Sam crawled inside the tent and sat next to him.

"Gee, Sam, shouldn't you be afraid someone will see you?"

"Why are you being so nasty?"

"Why didn't you stay with me overnight?"

"I thought you needed the rest."

"You're a lousy liar."

"What makes you think that's a lie? Dev, you were so exhausted and bruised, I just wanted you to sleep and recover."

The rage vanished from Dev. "I'm sorry. I think I'm just angry at myself. I needed you here, Sam. I wanted to hold you in my arms. To make me feel safe after what happened."

"I'm sorry, Devlin. It seems I can't make a good decision when it comes to us."

Facing Sam full on, Dev asked sheepishly, "How bad do I look?"

Brushing back Dev's hair from his forehead, Sam answered, "Not too bad."

"Black and blue?"

"No." Sam touched the small split in Dev's lip.

"Swollen?"

"Only slightly."

Dev felt for the edge of the band-aid on his eyebrow and peeled it off painfully. "How about this one?"

"Just a slit. You should keep something on it."

"Bruised?"

Sam inspected it. "No."

"So, all in all I don't look like a train wreck?"

A sensuous smile appeared on Sam's face. "You look rugged, masculine, and like a real macho mother-fucker."

"Shut up!" Dev laughed shyly. "You make me want to fight again just to turn you on."

The smile quickly faded. "You fighting does not turn me on."

"I see you already showered and shaved." Dev tried not to be so hurt by Sam's innocent actions.

"I did. I was really reluctant to wake you. I know how bad you felt last night."

Motivating himself to sit up, Dev looked down at his exposed chest. Touching all his scrapes and scratches softly, he sighed, "What's my back look like?"

When he twisted around, Sam caressed him soothingly. "You're a bit battered back here."

"It's from the damn brick wall."

"Are you going to tell me exactly how it happened? Or should I just assume you mouthed off?"

Meeting Sam's brown eyes, Dev did not want to tell him the truth. He didn't know why, but something made him reluctant. Maybe it was because of Tony and their kiss. Dev felt like he had cheated, but he and Sam weren't even a committed couple at the moment, were they? "Mouthing off."

"I figured. I'll wait outside while you get ready. Okay?"

"Okay." After Sam crept out of the tent, Dev tried not to feel guilty. He located clean clothing and his toiletries bag.

Standing up in broad daylight and the passing throng, Dev wondered if Sam was being straight with him about his appearance. Knowing he'd find out soon enough, he said, "I'll be right back," to Sam and headed to the showers.

A line had formed. As he stood waiting, Dev peeked at himself in the mirrors over the sink. Licking at the split in his lip, Dev found an older man staring at him with a knowing smirk.

"Bar brawl?"

"Yeah." Dev followed him as they moved up in the line.

"I heard there was a good fight at one in Sturgis. Cops arrested a handful. You at that one?"

Knowing others were listening, Dev went along. "Yes. I got out before they showed."

"What was it about?"

"No clue. Fists just started flying."

"You look all right. I heard some were hospitalized."

Dev touched his lip again. "Not too obvious?"

"I wouldn't worry. Chicks dig men who fight."

"I'm so glad." Dev gave him a big cheesy grin.

Finally under a hot spray of water, Dev had a good look in the bright light at his body. Light scratches seemed to be everywhere on him and his knuckles were cut from one of the fuckers' teeth where he punched him in the mouth. Not to mention, he felt achy all over.

Dried, dressed, and leaning over a sink to shave, Dev took a closer look at the cut on his eyebrow and agreed with Sam that he should keep something on it for another day or so. It was gaping open and Dev wanted it sealed shut.

~

Sam waited, sitting by their bikes. He hoped that now that Dev had been in a battle, he got it out of his system and they could finally relax. Seeing Dev approach made his heart skip a beat. Sam stood, salivating as he watched Dev's strut in his tight jeans and white cotton tank.

"I do need to cover this cut again." Dev pointed to his eyebrow.

"You want me to do it?"

"If you wouldn't mind. The men's toilet is packed at the moment and I don't want to go wait on line again just to stand at a sink and mirror."

Sam watched as Dev threw his towel and kit into his tent, returning with the small red box.

"Sit down." Sam gestured to the grassy spot.

Kneeling in front of Dev, Sam squeezed a dab of ointment on the pad of the adhesive strip and held it aloft.

"Try and close the cut."

"I will." Sam pressed it to Dev's skin, pushing the slice together.

"Thanks."

Staring at Dev's sad eyes, Sam imagined pulling him close for a reassuring kiss. Yes, it did suck that he couldn't. He wouldn't dare. Not now. Not after the pounding Dev took.

"No problem. Ready to eat?" Sam handed Dev back the first aid box.

After Dev stuck it into his tent, he nodded. "Yeah."

Finding the church pancake breakfast, Sam followed Dev down the long buffet line and filled his plate with food.

They took a seat next to each other and across from some older men wearing wedding rings who were presumably with their wives. Sam greeted them softly and began eating his food. "What's on the agenda today?" he asked Dev.

"I was thinking of going home."

Spinning around to stare at Dev, Sam choked, "Are you serious?"

"Yes."

"No, come on, Dev. Do you feel that bad? I thought you seemed okay this morning. Are you in pain?"

Dev continued to eat in silence.

"Dev? We could get out of here for a nice leisurely ride to Spearfish Canyon."

"I already did."

"When?"

"When you left me in Sturgis yesterday."

Feeling crushed, Sam ate more slowly, losing his appetite. "I don't want you to go."

After a deep exhale of breath, Dev asked quietly, "What are we doing here, Sam? We have no interest in the damn wet T-shirt contests, and the music sucks."

"There are fire dancers later tonight."

"Ooh!" Dev replied sarcastically.

"Wow. Whatever happened last night, really affected you." Sam tried to understand where Dev was coming from. Perhaps if he had his ass kicked, he'd be pining for home as well. He just didn't want Dev to leave. He wanted to stay with him.

"You have no idea." Dev continued to eat.

"Seriously?" Sam asked, "So much so you'd leave even though you paid until Sunday morning?"

"Who cares?"

"I do."

Dev met his gaze.

"If you leave, I'm going as well. But think about it for a little while. Maybe you'll feel better after the meal and some time to relax." Sam snuck his hand on Dev's leg for a second before he drew it back.

~

Dev's fear was of seeing Tony. Physically he was feeling okay, all things considered. He was just torn between fucking Tony's brains out and having homicidal thoughts of revenge. And it was screwing with Dev's head. He didn't want to say a word about it to Sam. Dev was trying to convince himself that he and Sam were nothing more than a fling so far. They just met, had two bouts of sex, and at the moment weren't even seeing eye to eye. In Dev's book that did not a relationship make. It was a prelude to one, possibly, or so he hoped. Or it was just some fun and games during Sturgis. Once they returned to Centerville and went about their own lives, Dev had no idea what Sam's thoughts would be on continuing to date and socialize. The madness that surrounded them wasn't conducive to a good, solid beginning. Dev was painfully aware of that fact.

And Dev wasn't so sure he was ready for a commitment anyway. He'd had a seven-year marriage and that didn't turn into anything even close to "'til death do us part". More like "until you figure out who the hell you are do us part".

"Please, Dev. Stay with me."

"Why do you want to stay? What are you getting out of this?" Dev finished his food and set his fork down on his plate.

"A once in a lifetime experience, that's what. I don't want to remember it for leaving early or having a lousy time. I want to look back on this as the riding rally of a lifetime. Dev, you do realize some of these individuals are really making the most of it."

"I know. I can't wait for the next dill pickle suck-off contest."

Sam laughed shyly. "Look. I know you had a really bad experience, and if you want to leave, I'll go home with you. It's up to you."

Rubbing his forehead as he considered it, Dev gave in. "Okay. I'll stay." Dev felt he owed Sam that. After all.

"Cool." Sam ate with renewed gusto.

~

They spent the day on the bikes riding through the Black Hills to Lead and on to Deadwood. Dev thought the town looked like a fake television set for *Rawhide*. But Sam was lapping it up, so he tried to be on his best behavior. Anything to get out of the claustrophobic sensation the camp gave him and get something other than pizza and tacos to eat for dinner.

They dined at a steak house while they were on the road and returned at dusk. Once again waiting in the long queue at the gate for entry, Dev rolled his bike up with Sam behind him. It was overcast and slightly cooler, with the wind once again blowing in strong gusts.

Showing their bracelet ID and gaining entry, Dev rode to their site and parked, glad to get off the bike again for the night. As he removed his helmet and jacket, Sam did the same next to him.

"Do you feel up to seeing the fire troupe dancers?" Sam asked.

"You know it'll be hokey." Dev tucked his leather jacket into his saddlebag.

"So what? Come on."

"Let me change into my jeans." Dev crawled into his tent and yanked off his leather pants. Once he was horizontal it took all his effort to dress and go back out. Sleep sounded so nice at the moment.

Lying down to zipper and button his fly, Dev put his shoes back on and climbed out of his tent. Folding his leather pants, he wedged them into the saddlebag, locking it and then their two bikes together as well.

Taking out his mobile phone, Dev turned it on and noticed he had a message. While he waited for Sam who was inside his tent changing, he heard his mother's voice.

"Please use common sense there, Devlin. Listen to your father. I love you. Call us when you get a chance."

Shutting it off, Dev slipped it into his pocket again, knowing her warning was too late.

Sam emerged from his tent, smiling at him affectionately.

Lapping up the adoration, Dev gave Sam's torn jeans a good once over. "Only pair you brought?"

"Yes."

"Those holes are getting bigger." Dev had to cross his arms over his chest and trap his hands to prevent his urge to grope Sam's body hungrily.

"Are they?" Sam peered down at them, continuing to lock up his leather clothing.

"What will you do when they become obscene?"

"They won't."

Instantly turned on, Dev couldn't tear his eyes away from Sam's exposed thigh. "Are you naked under them?" he whispered.

"Yes." Sam gave Dev that hot flirtatious grin that drove him wild.

Moaning in agony, Dev play-acted he was in pain.

"Later."

"Always later."

Pocketing his keys, Sam replied, "Yes. But I do come through for you, don't I?"

"With flying colors." Dev drew near to get a sniff of him.

"Then don't complain."

"I'll try not to." Dev noticed a small worn spot in the denim on Sam's butt as well, soon, with any luck, to become threadbare. Dev turned his back to the flow of pedestrians and stuffed his hand into his own pants to adjust himself.

"Already hard?" Sam asked.

"As a rock. You have the effect on me, Rhodes. Insta-wood. "

"You know I'm flattered. Just be patient and you'll be amply rewarded. I promise. Am I right? In private later? I'm assuming you learned your lesson."

"Yes, Dad." Dev rolled his eyes.

"Right. Let's find the fire dancers."

"After you." Dev bowed, licking his chops at the chance of getting at him again later that evening.

~

The pounding amplified beat of the rock band in Memorial Stage echoed off the flat landscape.

Dev sipped his third beer and was finally feeling a nice buzz. The fire routine was amusing, but not as captivating as Sam anticipated. Another lewd contest with drunken tattooed women was going on behind them. Dev and Sam attempted to enjoy themselves in peace, sipping their brews and talking together quietly.

"So, tell me about your writing?" Sam sucked on the neck of his beer bottle, gulping down the contents. When he was done, he licked his lips in a sexy tease.

Dev was happy to see Sam finally letting down his guard a little. "I write erotic gay fiction."

"No!" Sam's eyes lit up.

"Yes."

"Holy shit. You said thrillers, didn't you?"

"You really think I want to go around announcing what I write? Come on, Sam." Dev peered back at the stage area. Men were hosing down women in T-shirts.

"I can't wait to read one."

"Good. Buy all of them. Tell all your friends." Dev laughed, setting his bottle down on the bar in front of him.

"I've got a good buzz."

"I can tell," Dev replied, smiling.

"You?"

"Getting there."

"Where do you think everyone from our club ended up tonight?" Sam leaned heavily against the counter they were standing at.

"All over. There are so many different events around. My guess is most of them are at the music concert."

"I just don't know any of the bands. Who are Staind?"

"You're asking me?" Dev laughed. "You want another beer?"

"I shouldn't." Sam appeared tempted.

"One more?" Dev slid money on the bar.

"One more. Then that's it."

Dev waited for the bartender's attention and asked for another round. Thanking him, Dev handed Sam his fourth bottle. "So, tell me about what you like to do besides design websites."

Taking a drink first, Sam shrugged. "I don't know."

"You belong to a gym?"

"No. I run, bike...I don't really get into the gym thing. You?"

142

"Yes. Dad and I go every morning. He got me into lifting weights."

"I can tell. Christ, you're really built, Dev."

Dev looked around discretely. "That was bold of you."

"That's why I don't want to get drunk."

"Why? I like you horny."

"Be quiet."

Dev chuckled, glancing again at the stage. Some women were stripped from the waist up while the crowd screamed in delight as the contest continued. "I wish they would have shows like that with pretty boys in soaked g-strings."

"Me too."

Dev checked his watch, it was nearing eleven thirty and the sky was finally getting pitch dark. Craning his neck up at it, Dev couldn't catch many stars through the bright lights of the campsite.

"What do you want to do after this?" Sam asked, slightly slurring his words.

"Go back to the tents. I'm exhausted."

"Good. I was hoping you'd say that. How are you feeling? Sore?"

Dev leaned close to whisper, "I feel fine. Are we going to fool around?"

"Why not?" Sam grinned wickedly.

Winking back, yearning for Sam's naked skin against his own, Dev finished his beer quickly. Checking out the finalists of the contest curiously, he noticed typically it was the largest ladies of the group.

Sam set his bottle down. "Ready?"

"Yes. Let me just leave the guy a tip." Dev found a few singles as Sam did the same.

They walked back to the camping grounds leisurely. As they passed, Dev looked at all the sideshows. It was pretty much the same all over.

"I need a piss. Too much beer," Sam announced.

"You want to go into one here? Or wait until we get to our campsite?"

"Here."

"Okay."

"You have to go?"

"Not yet."

"Be right back."

Dev nodded, standing outside the port-o-potties.

A roaring cheer rang out from the Memorial Stage area. Dev assumed it was for the band. All he could hear from where they were was a deep bass sound, throbbing like a jungle beat. Dev felt tired, but knew he'd get his second wind when he and Sam were snuggling together in his cozy tent.

Sam emerged, joining Dev on their stroll once more. After ten minutes they made it to their home away from home in the midst of so many large canopies.

"Your place or mine?" Sam asked seductively.

"Oh, crap. Hang on. Let me buy another condom." Dev took change out of his pocket.

"I'll be waiting."

Acknowledging him, Dev headed to the restroom building close by. While he was inside, he relieved himself and as he washed his hands he checked out his cuts in the mirror. Purchasing two of the most lubricated condoms they supplied, he stuffed them into his jeans' pocket and left.

Just as he was exiting, he spotted his nemesis. Instantly a surge of rage washed over him. Dev bolted to catch up to him and grabbed him from behind, forcing him to into the darkness at the rear of the restroom building.

The suddenness of the attack caught Tony off guard. It wasn't until he had his back to the wall that he realized what was going on. "Get off me!"

Dev snarled, "You son of a bitch! You left me to defend myself against those two maniacs!"

"Looks like you lived," Tony snapped.

Dev crushed him against the bricks and mortar. "No thanks to you. How could you do that to me? How could you tell them I tried to rape you, you idiot! They wanted to kill me."

"Let go of me!" Tony tried to twist away.

"No! At least apologize. For Christ's sake, Tony, I swear I thought I was dead."

"I wish you were dead. Get AIDS and die!"

Dev grabbed Tony under his jaw. Tony's knee came up towards Dev's balls. Dev twisted his hips, avoiding the shot. "You can't fool me any longer, Spagna. I know your fucking secret. You goddamn closet queen."

"Get your fucking faggot hands off me!"

Dev connected to Tony's mouth. The jolt of electricity that zapped through Dev astonished him. Though Tony allowed Dev's tongue to enter his mouth, Tony battled to get Dev off.

When he finally succeeded in throwing Dev back from him, they were both panting in fury.

"Keep lying to yourself, asshole," Dev mocked.

"You stay the fuck away from me." Tony pointed his index finger into Dev's face.

Dev snatched it out of the air and sucked it.

An animalistic, euphoric moan erupted from Tony, until he jerked his hand away and took a swing at Dev's face.

Avoiding it, Dev rammed Tony back against the dark wall painfully, hearing the breath leak out of Tony's lungs from the impact. Dev groped Tony's crotch to see if he had a hard-on. A huge erect cock was under Tony's denim zipper. "Jesus! Admit this excites you, you moron."

"Will you leave me the fuck alone?" Tony ranted and pushed Dev back. "I swear I'm going to kill you. Stay the fuck away from me before I get your ass kicked again. Worse this time."

As Tony vanished into the darkness, Dev took a moment to catch his breath.

~

Sam waited. Just about to go look for Dev inside the men's toilet, he spotted him coming towards him.

"You okay?"

"I thought you were going to be waiting inside your tent." Dev shoved him towards it.

"I was. What the hell's wrong with you?" Sam regained his balance.

"Get in!" Dev ordered.

Hesitating, checking the area, Sam was shocked when Dev pushed him again. "Hey!"

"Stop looking around and get the fuck inside."

"Jesus!" Sam knelt down to open the zipper of his tent. Before he was even all the way in, Dev was behind him urging him to hurry. Sitting back to gape at Dev in awe, Sam couldn't figure out where the calm man he had been drinking with went. "Did something happen?"

Once Dev closed them inside, in the dim light from a spotlight shining from the restrooms, he began tearing at Sam's clothing.

Choking at the intensity, Sam hurried to assist before his torn jeans became unwearable rags. Naked from the waist down, Sam didn't get a chance to remove his shirt before Dev had his penis out of his pants, a condom on, and was moving toward Sam to get in. The excitement in Sam was making him dizzy. He loved rough play and though he hadn't discussed it with Dev in the crowded surroundings of the event, Sam preferred it that way.

Staring at Dev's body language, the power and masculinity of his actions, Sam was in heat. His dick had gone as stiff as a pole and his heart rate soared in anticipation. Gaping in awe at the big erection protruding from Dev's zipper, Sam wanted to reach out for it, stroke it, suck it, but Dev was taking control of this scene and had a different plan.

Dev forced Sam's legs back to his chest, penetrating his ass with abandon and pumping hard. Sam couldn't catch his astonished breath.

In reflex, as if Sam anticipated pain, he cringed at the force with only the rubber for lubrication. Though it was rough, it wasn't unbearable. Finally Sam was able to choke out a few words. "Holy shit, Devlin! What's the rush?"

"Oh, Christ, hang on… I'm there..." A final deep thrust and Dev came, throwing back his head, gasping and closing his eyes tightly.

Before Sam even had a chance to breathe, Dev had pulled out and dropped down between Sam's thighs.

It was happening too quickly. Sam imagined a long slow screw, with an hour of erotic foreplay. It appeared his lover had an opposite agenda. And though it wasn't Sam's original plan, he was savoring the burst of pleasure that rocked through his loins.

Shivers raced over Sam's skin and his balls tightened, pre-blast off. "Slow down. I don't want to come yet."

As if he were lost in a dream, Dev was sucking deep and fast, moaning too loudly for Sam's liking, but the excitement soon outweighed the fear. Forcing his eyes open, Sam looked at Dev's face. The nirvana-like expression sent him over the edge. *"Oh, God! Oh, my fucking God..."* Arching his back, Sam came, biting down on his lip to prevent more loud expletives of ecstasy from passing through his teeth.

As if the taste of his come had sent Dev into the stratosphere, he drew every last drop out of Sam's cock, milking it, sucking deep, slow and hard, his hands gripped to the base as he did.

Gasping to gain air into his laboring lungs, Sam's body was vibrating from the intensity of the climax, and Dev obviously had no desire to stop sucking. Staring at the dark tent ceiling, his heart beating through his ribs like a kettledrum, Sam's knees were bent in a wide straddle as Dev continued to throat him slow and deep, lapping his tongue up and down his length. It felt so incredible, Sam didn't want him to stop. The raw desire that Dev showed for him was making Sam fall so madly in love he was overwhelmed.

Swallowing audibly, Sam listened to the noise around them, that continuous amplified rumbling bass traveling across the flat plain, the voices of drunken wild parties and Harley's revving.

It was an orgy of decadence. Normal business men and women set free to pretend they were teenagers and sex gods. Who was he to deny he wasn't a party to it all? Inside this private domain, Sam was. Secret, hidden from view, he and his lover could be themselves. And the wild attraction he felt for Dev was turning him on so much, Sam never wanted it to end.

As that slow lapping was bringing back the fire in him, Sam felt a ripple of pleasure stir between his legs. Leaning up, Sam caught Dev, removing the spent condom from his cock finally and dropping it without looking, out of their way. As Dev made himself more comfortable, resting between Sam's thighs, Dev stepped up the level again of his sucking.

Dropping back, closing his eyes, Sam drifted with Dev's tongue as it drew circles around the head of his cock and into his slit. One warm hand released the base of his dick and began kneading his balls, stroking between his legs. It was so sensual, Sam felt another ripple of pleasure and elevated his hips to rise with it.

And as if it were a sign to let Dev know he was back on track for number two, Dev moaned in longing, sucking down to the root of Sam's penis. At the depth of penetration, Sam quivered in delight. "*Oh, Dev…*" he hissed softly.

Kneeling up, trying to get better access, Dev smoothed his hands all over Sam's body, pushing up his shirt, running his fingers back down Sam's thighs and again onto his balls.

A shooting spark of pleasure rushed up Sam's body as Dev's hands fondled him in all the right spots. He released a grunt unintentionally, biting his lip to prevent another that might expose what they were doing inside this tiny tent.

The sound caused Dev to work in earnest. Rocking as he drew Sam's cock in and out of his mouth, Dev began masturbating.

Hearing him, Sam leaned up to look. in the dim shadows, the sight of that fantastic man sucking him, Dev's forehead furrowed with his pleasure, his eyes closed, and his right hand jerking himself off, Sam thought he was going to explode. Dev was his living fantasy, the man of his dreams, and to see Dev getting off so wildly on sucking his cock was incredible. Sam couldn't explain why it felt right between them, he only knew it did. Sex like this, the animal attraction, the feeling of being united as one, it was liberating in its sense of abandon.

Unable to prevent it, Sam felt his balls tense up, his cock go solid, throbbing like mad. Gritting his jaw on a scream of euphoria, Sam's body clenched and shot out its load again, the

149

sensation feeling as if it was prolonged by multiple orgasms. Flopping back to the floor and spinning in delirium as it rushed up his spine, Sam had to chew on his knuckle to quiet his whimpering groans.

A second later Sam felt hot come spatter his body and had to grip the sleeping bag under him in desperation he was so keyed up from the act.

As he recovered, gasping for breath, Sam felt Dev licking him clean. His lungs working on overdrive, Sam had to lie still trying to recuperate. Dev's lips and tongue efficiently removed any mess. Once Dev sat back on his heels to wipe the sweat off his face, Sam reached out and yanked him down on top of him, wrapping his naked legs around Dev's denim ones and finding Dev's mouth. He was so mad for Dev he wanted to show him just how much.

Through their panting breaths, Sam kissed him, gripping him close, running his hands through Dev's hair. "You hot son of a bitch! You fantastic, hot son of a bitch!" Sam hissed as quietly as he could.

An exhausted chuckle escaped Dev.

"Strip and lie with me." Sam pushed at Dev's shirt.

"You...you want me to stay here?" Dev panted for breath. "I figured you'd kick me out. It's got to be nearing midnight."

Sam was torn in half. "Christ, Dev, why did we meet now?"

"How else could we have met?" Dev leaned up on his elbows.

"I don't know. I'm just glad we have."

"So? What's the deal? Am I staying or going?"

After a pause, Sam fought so hard with his inner monologue, begging to be strong and not upset Dev. But in the end, his paranoia and Dev's gay-bashing won out. "I'm sorry."

"I figured." Dev zipped up his jeans.

"You angry?" Sam reached out to touch him.

"A little."

"Dev, please try and understand."

"I do. See ya in the morning." Dev opened the flap.

"See ya."

As Dev disappeared, Sam could hear the tent next to him opening. He wanted nothing more than to sleep with Dev overnight. It was torture not to. To watch him leave, feel the loneliness of the solitude after a sexual bout so incredible it left him speechless. But it was only a couple more days. When they got home they could be themselves. Sam promised himself would make it up to Dev when they were back in Ohio.

Rolling to his side, Sam wished he had courage to call Dev back, but like the Cowardly Lion, he needed to find it in Oz.

chapter Nine

Dev woke to Sam calling his name outside his tent.

"You awake?"

Trying not to be disappointed with Sam's reluctance to sleep with him overnight in his tent, Dev moaned, "Yeah."

"Want to come to the showers with me?"

Dev perked up. Poking his head out of the tent he asked, "You want me to shower with you?"

"You never stop." Sam stared at him, his towel and toiletry bag in hand. "One day, Dev. One more day."

"All right," Dev assented, "let me get ready. Hang on."

As they walked to the building together, Dev couldn't help but recall his face burrowed between Sam's legs. Leaning closer to him Dev hissed, "Last night..." in Sam's ear.

A soft, shy chuckle was his reply. When Dev peered over at Sam, Sam was beaming at him. The sight of Sam's adoring smile sent chills over Dev's body. Instantly he was in heat.

Once again going through the routine of waiting for a shower, shaving, and trying not to ogle each other, Dev finished up his morning regiment and met Sam back at their campsite.

"They're actually having machinegun shooting today," Sam chuckled, draping his wet towel over his tent.

"Perfect," Dev replied, laughing.

"You're looking better. You're healing quickly. I forgot about that lip last night when we were kissing. Did it hurt?" Sam peeked around, adding, "You know, while you were sucking me off?"

"A little. It was worth it. Believe me."

When Sam reached out to touch his cut mouth, Dev narrowed his eyes at him. "I don't get you."

"What?" Sam dropped his hand.

"You sometimes do things in public that are controversial, and yet you don't let me."

"Don't start. Haven't you already been beaten up enough for your 'controversy'?"

Dev was left with that bad taste in his mouth again at their head banging over this same topic.

As they walked, brushing shoulders occasionally, to get their breakfast, Dev wanted to tell Sam what really happened that night, to be honest and open. But his attraction for Tony, the closet queen, was preventing him. Especially after last night and his and Sam's incredible sexual bout.

Meeting up with Jerry and the gang, Dev set his plate of pancakes and sausages in front of him and met Tony's angry glare. Smiling demonically in return, knowing his dirty little secret, Dev ate his food and imagined planting another good smack on Tony's handsome face, and he didn't mean with his hand.

Sam caught the two of them in a staring match. Nudging Dev, Sam warned, "Don't start. You two will be at it in minutes."

Grinning at Tony's snarl, Dev wondered what going *at it* with Tony would be like.

153

It seemed Dev won the contest of wills because Tony stood up and left the table without a word.

June asked, "Is he okay?"

Ralph replied, "He's been moody. I think he's getting grief from the wife. She keeps calling."

"Oh, dear." June shook her head.

Dev wondered what the woman would do if she knew of Tony's infidelity with the biker babes and his inner desire to swap spit with another man.

"I feel sorry for her." Sam ate another bite of his pancake.

"I feel sorry for him," Dev added, much to Sam's seeming bewilderment. "What time are we heading out tomorrow, Jerry?" Dev asked.

"Early. The earlier the better. I don't know about you boys, but I'm ready to be home. I've had enough."

They all nodded in agreement.

"At least I can say I was here," Sam commented. "I suppose there's bragging rights."

"We have other events, boys," Jerry addressed Sam and Dev. "We do local charity rides, and some day trips. I hope you two didn't join just for this event."

Immediately Sam kissed up. "No. I'm going to be involved, Jerry. I would like to do some shorter rides as well."

"Devlin?" Jerry inquired.

"Hm?" Dev wiped his mouth with his napkin. "Yeah, sure."

"When the hell did you get that cut over your eye?" Ralph pointed. "You weren't in that brawl over in Sturgis, were you?"

Dev caught Sam's gaze first. "Uh, yes. I was. Just got caught up in the melee."

"I warned everyone to be careful. I suppose it wasn't your fault though," Jerry added.

"No. Believe me, Jerry, it was not my fault."

"Well, I'm glad you're all right. Rumor is that some of the guys were sent to the hospital and jail."

"I heard the same thing," Dev replied.

"Well, I'm off to watch the machine-gunning event." Jerry rose up.

As the others followed, Dev looked back at Sam.

"Is that your story?" Sam asked.

"Yes."

"I suppose it's less 'controversial'."

"Ya think?" Dev rolled his eyes at the folly.

"Okay, forget it. Where to?" Sam stood and tossed his paper plate into the trash.

"I suppose the machinegun thing." Dev rose up off the bench.

"You know, there are going to be cowboys in an event tonight. There's quick-draw shoot out, or something like that."

"About time. I love cowboys." Dev grinned wickedly.

"You'll have to tell me all of your erotic fantasies one day."

"Just buy my books," Dev chuckled as he left the area. Hearing Sam laughing as he followed, Dev grinned happily.

~

By eight in the evening, Dev and Sam found a spot to watch the quick-shooting event. Ralph noticed them and joined them in the bleachers. Dev looked around for Tony. "Where's your friend?" Dev asked.

"He went home."

"What?" Dev gaped in surprise.

"He left this morning after breakfast."

Sam sighed with relief. "Good."

"No kidding?" Dev leaned closer to Ralph, over Sam. "Did he say why?"

"Like I said this morning, I think his wife was driving him crazy. We talked a lot about it. I told him if he's not happy with her he should leave her."

"Is he?"

"What do you care?" Sam asked.

"Just curious."

"I don't know," Ralph replied. "I think he has a lot of pressure from both their families. He told me they're very religious practicing Catholics and divorce is one of those things that are frowned upon."

Dev absorbed the details. It certainly made sense as to why Tony was so deep in the closet.

"So, what's this Buffalo Bill show about?" Sam asked.

"Some sharpshooter who pops balloons as he rides his horse," Ralph laughed.

"Oh." Sam turned to Dev and relayed, "No cowboys."

Dev shrugged thinking about Tony.

~

Over a beer in one of the crowded bars, Sam asked, "Anything you want to do tonight?"

"We've seen and done it all." Dev sipped his drink.

"You've been very quiet today."

"I'm ready to go home."

"I know. Me too. I'm just dreading the long ride on that bike. My ass is finally feeling okay."

Dev shrugged.

"Are you mad at me?"

"What?" Dev met Sam's chocolate brown eyes. "Mad at you?"

After he looked around, Sam whispered, "You want me to follow you home tomorrow? Give you a nice ass rub? With my tongue?"

"That's an offer that's too good to refuse!" Dev lit up.

"No, seriously, Dev, you want to keep seeing each other?"

After another drink of his beer, Dev asked, "Do you?"

"Yes."

Surprised at his confidence, Dev replied. "Okay."

"That was rather lukewarm."

"Was it? I didn't mean it to be."

"I'm not an idiot, Dev. I know how annoyed you've been with me throughout this event."

"I'm not annoyed anymore. I get it."

"You did get it. You probably needed a stitch in your eyebrow you got it so well."

Dev instantly remembered Tony's hot kiss.

"Dev, I'm trying not to have expectations. I just think on different terms we may have a better chance at a relationship. Certainly not here in this artificial environment."

Looking around them in exaggeration of checking out the area, Dev teased, "You sure you want to talk about that here?"

"Shut up," Sam laughed.

"What are you looking for, Sam?"

"I don't know. I suppose a steady thing."

"Exclusive?"

"Eventually. If it's right."

Nodding, sucking down more beer, Dev asked, "How do you know if something's right?"

"I suppose it evolves."

"Can I say something?"

At the odd comment, Sam looked around for a second, leaned closer and said, "Yes."

"You've been burned, haven't you?"

Reacting in surprise, Sam sat up, staring at Dev.

"Thought so." Dev finished his beer.

"Am I that transparent?"

"That cautious."

"No. I'm cautious because I'm here."

"Believe what you want." Dev looked back at yet another lewd contest involving intoxicated women in scant leather garments.

"Christ, I had no idea I was broadcasting my insecurity."

"Like you're on a PA system, Sam."

"Is that what's turning you off me?"

"It ain't a turn on," Dev replied, adding, "but you certainly are. You get me into heat just looking at you." Dev's eyes lowered to that gaping hole in Sam's threadbare denims. It had most definitely grown in the last few days. "I just wish you had bigger balls, and I'm not referring to your anatomy. Believe me, you're hung like a fucking horse." Predictably, Sam glanced around in fear.

Dev threw up his hands in frustration. He was so tired of Sam's paranoia, he could scream. With nothing else to amuse him, he looked back at the stage as women became more obscene.

"Please," Sam begged, "tomorrow I'll be a different person. I just really don't want my face rearranged into a Picasso painting."

"Why not? Didn't do me any harm."

"Didn't it? After an attempted rape? You wanted to go running home. Who are you kidding? I beg to differ." Sam looked at the stage, quickly turning back to Dev. "You didn't see the state you were in that night. And besides that, Devlin, you've got fifty fucking pounds of muscle on me. I wouldn't have been able to win the battle I'm guessing you were in."

"I do not. Shut the fuck up." Dev laughed.

"Oh? How much do you weigh?" Sam urged.

"Two ten."

"Holy fuck! I'm only one eighty and we're the same fucking height."

"That's only thirty pounds, so you're wrong." Dev tipped his bottle up for the last drop.

"Pure muscle, Dev, you're pure, solid muscle." Sam gazed at Dev's chest hungrily.

"Shut up, you're making me horny." When Sam raised his head to scan the surroundings, Dev grabbed his jaw. "Stop looking around!"

Jerking back from his hands, Sam glared at him. "Cut it out. I'm too tired for any more crap. Let's go."

"Tired of fat chicks flashing their tits?" Dev jeered, trailing behind Sam as he left the bar.

~

Once they had washed up for the night, and reclined outside the tents to enjoy the breeze, Sam felt he could relax.

He wanted to keep seeing Dev after they got home, but something about Dev's cavalier attitude raised up the caution sign. Perhaps Dev wasn't ready to settle down.

Rolling to his side, Sam propped his chin in his palm and asked, "After your divorce, did you ever get involved in a serious relationship with a man?"

"No."

"Just screwed around?"

"Pretty much."

Sam heard a woman's hyena laugh and imagined how drunk everyone around them was becoming. "So, am I to assume you wouldn't be ready for one now?"

Dev turned to look at Sam. "I don't know."

"Just haven't found the right man?" Sam asked sharply, torturing himself.

"I'd leap on you and prove you wrong right now if you weren't so fucking paranoid."

"Can I take a rain check on that? Say for about four o'clock tomorrow?"

Dev laughed softly.

Peering around in the darkness, Sam touched Dev's chest lightly.

"What are you doing?" Dev accused. "Someone will notice."

Sam retracted his hand.

"See? Sucks, doesn't it?"

"Yes."

"Welcome to my world."

"Dev, it's the real world."

Sitting up, Dev exclaimed, "Why do you care? You're self-employed, and single."

"Shh!" Sam waved at him. "Yes, that's me from the time we hit Dayton on. Not now."

"Augh! I swear I can't stand this." Dev went to stand.

Sam gripped his arm, stopping him. "Please! Dev."

Shoving Sam's hand off, Dev sat up and glared at him. "Just remember this when we're back in Dayton and you wonder why I'm so reluctant."

"Ouch! You don't mean that."

"Don't I?"

Sam didn't realize how much it would sting. "Why can't you understand?"

"I'm trying to. But all I see is a weak homosexual who's hiding."

"Jesus, Dev!"

"Never mind."

"Where are you going?"

"I need a walk to clear my head."

When he left, Sam was devastated. Why couldn't Dev see it was temporary? What was the big deal?

The pain in his chest at the thought of them never seeing each other after this was killing him. Dev was right. They should have gone home yesterday. What were they still doing here?

~

As he walked past the men's toilet, Dev recalled Tony and their confrontation. The passionate hatred morphing into lust. The heat of testosterone and sweat rushing up his nostrils. Tony's grip on his body, the size of his dick as it throbbed in Tony's jeans. It was like a brand burning on his brain, and Dev craved that kind of brute strength. Weakness annoyed him. There was nothing more repulsive to him than a wimp.

Strolling by tents loaded with boisterous campers, wasted on every type of chemical known to man, Dev wished Tony hadn't left. He would seek him out. They would battle, and he would get more of those kisses. Those hot Italian stallion kisses.

"Hey," a feminine voice crooned.

Dev noticed a woman in a leather halter top that was covered in metal studs and riding chaps over a pink bikini bottom, holding out a smoldering joint to him.

He approached her and took the joint. Taking a deep hit, he held it, handing it back. As he exhaled he coughed. It'd been since high school that he'd smoked pot.

"Wanna screw?"

"Me?" He laughed, pointing to his chest.

"Mm." She rested against his body, smoothing her hands over his shirt.

He took the joint out of her fingers and took another hit. As he smoked it, she ran her painted nails down his body. "I was second runner up, Miss Buffalo Chip."

"I'm so impressed," he mocked, smoking the joint without passing it to her.

"Most guys would kill to fuck me."

"Would they?" He offered the roach to her but she didn't reach for it. Inhaling, he finished it, tossing it aside. Once he held his breath as long as he could, he let go a thin stream of smoke into the night air.

"Yes," she hummed, cupping Dev's crotch. "How can you not be hard?"

"Gee? Am I not excited?" He acted surprised.

She stroked her hand all over his crotch. "What are you, impudent?"

"Impudent?" he choked with laughter.

Wrapping around him, she rubbed her breasts against his chest. It only made him laugh more.

"Kiss me."

"No thanks." He tilted his jaw away.

"Are you queer?"

"Completely."

As if she didn't hear right, she stared at him again, her mouth agape. "What?"

"What?" he mimicked. "Thanks for the toke, cutie."

"Wait. Don't go."

Winking at her, he continued on his walk, feeling high and very lonely.

~

Sam grew tired of waiting. Crawling into his tent, he lay back and sighed deeply. It was his fault. He knew it. He should just throw caution to the wind and be himself. So what if he took a beating?

"Uh, no way." Though he wished he could be Mr. Macho and enjoy a good fight, he never had. His brother was the real man of the family. Tough, rock hard, fearless. Not him. No. Just seeing the bruises and cuts on Dev made him wince. He certainly did not want to take a licking and prove something to someone. He knew who he was. He wasn't ashamed to be gay. On the contrary. But he also knew there was a time for being out, and a time for being private. He just wished they could be home. He didn't like this hiding game anymore than Dev did.

Curling up on his sleeping bag, he hoped Dev joined him when he returned, but knew he wouldn't.

~

An hour later Dev stood in front of both tents. He assumed Sam was already asleep in his own, tired of waiting for him. Taking a coin out of his pocket, Dev flipped it, catching it and looking at the face. Heads, you lose. He entered his own tent alone, curling up, feeling heartsick, and tried to sleep.

chapter Ten

Early the next morning, Dev packed his clothing and dismantled his tent. Sam was doing the same, and though they weren't talking, Dev couldn't decide if it was because they were busy, or mad at each other. And if Sam was mad. Why? Because Dev hadn't crawled into his tent? After all the paranoia and conditions on their contact? Screw that. Life was too short.

Jerry appeared on his cruiser with June on the back. "You boys almost ready?"

"Yes," Dev answered, securing the straps on his sleeping bag and tent. After another look around the area to make sure they had everything, Dev stared at Sam. "You ready?"

He nodded, not making eye contact.

Placing his helmet on his head, Dev straddled his bike, starting it up.

Rolling behind Jerry and June, Dev peered behind him to see Sam, Doug, and Ralph riding in single file out of the madness and hopefully back to the real world.

Dev was very glad to be going home. He wished the memories of Sturgis had been what they were before he came,, a

164

crazy adventure for a teenage boy. Now? It left a sour taste in his mouth.

~

Finally back on the interstate, Dev began to feel those same sore spots torturing his body. It was time to get off this bike and get back to his routine of working out with his dad, writing and relaxing on his deck.

Glancing in his side mirror, he noticed Sam lagging behind him. Moving to the left edge of the lane, Dev deliberately slowed down. Sam caught up instantly. They looked at each other through their bug-spattered face shields. An ache formed in Dev. He wanted him. *Face it, Dev, you know Sam is solid and stable. The perfect boyfriend. What on earth do you want Tony for? A married man in denial? That's just lust, nothing more.*

Cruising in their leathers at seventy-five miles an hour, Dev still managed to exchange a sweet smile with Sam. Yes, he'd see him socially. Why not? The guy was gorgeous and smart. *What's not to like?*

~

Taking a break at a rest stop as they met Interstate 75 and were about to descend the map into Ohio from Toledo, Sam shut off his ignition and climbed stiffly off the bike. Dev was waiting for him. Removing his helmet and tucking it under his arm, Sam joined him on the walk to the men's room.

When he met Dev's blue eyes he was surprised at the affection in them. "How's your ass?"

"Aching for your cock."

Sam was so relieved Dev still wanted him, he laughed in delight. "Get over here."

Seeing the stunned expression on Dev's face, Sam wrapped around him and brought him into a kiss, in front of Jerry, Ralph, Doug, a dozen strangers, and God.

When they parted Dev gasped, "What the fuck?"

"Welcome to the real world, Devlin." Sam was thrilled he could finally let down his guard. It had been hell keeping it up.

"Wow!" Dev held Sam's hand as they continued to the bathroom for a much needed pit stop.

~

Beaming as they walked back to their bikes together, Dev began to think there may be a future between he and Sam if Sam truly was stifling his behavior just for the event. While those thoughts passed through his mind, Sam put his arm around Dev's shoulder.

"Almost home." Sam smiled.

"I can't wait. I'm already dying."

"Want to come to my place?"

"Yes, but after I stop home and park the bike. I think I'll be driving my car for the next few days to recuperate."

"I'll be waiting." Sam kissed him passionately and placed his helmet back on his head.

Instantly turned on, Dev looked at the rest of their group. June was the only one smiling at them. The rest of the men either were avoiding looking, or too busy to care. His excitement to get home and have Sam as he was now, confident and bold, was making Dev ache for his arms.

Another few grueling hours on Interstate 75 and they finally diverted to 675 and were close to home. As they neared Centerville, the group began to fracture and wave goodbye as they went their separate ways. Sam followed Dev off the Wilmington Pike exit and they parted at Clyo and Bigger Road. Dev waved and received one back.

Slowing down, Dev hit his garage door opener and parked as it elevated. Rolling the bike into his garage, he shut it down, took off his helmet and exhaled in relief. Managing to dismount while his body was in agony, Dev stood on his two feet, pausing to feel steady while his legs continued to vibrate. They didn't stop overnight like they had on the way up, wanting to drive straight home. Though he was glad they did, it was murder.

Staring at the tent, the sleeping bag, knowing how much crap he had to unpack, Dev suddenly felt too exhausted for so much work.

Leaving it for the moment, he exited the garage, closed the door behind him, walking to the front entrance of his condo. Stopping at his mailbox, he unlocked it and gathered the wad of paper, climbing the stairs to his abode, more exhausted by the moment.

Unlocking his front door, Dev entered, feeling grateful to be home again. As he stood in the hall, he dumped the mail on a counter, unzipped his leather jacket, peeled it off of his sweat-soaked shirt, and hung it in his closet. Leaning against the wall, he tugged off his boots, dragging his leather pants down his legs. Stripped down to his socks, and briefs, Dev moaned in agony at how much he ached. Walking to his bedroom, rubbing his sore balls, Dev stood near his nightstand and picked up his cordless phone, dialing.

"Hello?"

"Hi, Dad. I'm home."

"I'm glad you made it in one piece."

"I'm not sure. I think I left one of my nuts on the highway."

His father laughed. "Everything go okay?"

Dev heard his mother shouting in the background, "Is that Devlin?"

"Yes, Melinda," his father answered. Soon after, his mother picked up an extension.

"Hello, baby."

"Hi, Mom."

"Did it all work out for you?"

"Pretty much." Dev stretched his back and ran his hand over his aching ass muscles.

"What happened with the young man you met?" his father enquired.

"We had some great sex. He lives close by so we'll probably continue to get together."

"I'm so glad you're home," Melinda sighed.

"Me too, Mom. Anyway, I just now walked through the door. I need a shower and I may see Sam later if I'm up to it."

"Are you coming over tomorrow?" Jan asked. "We'll have a barbeque. Ask Sam over."

"I'll let you know."

"Okay, talk to you soon."

"See ya." Dev hung up, stripped off his briefs and socks and headed to the shower.

After he had washed up, Dev stretched out on his bed with the window open, feeling a cool breeze on his damp skin. Yearning to call Sam and cuddle with him, he wanted to desperately but ended up closing his eyes and falling asleep.

~

The telephone woke him. Groggy and disoriented, Dev picked it up. "Hello?"

"Hey."

"Hi, Sam." Dev rolled over and yawned.

"Are you coming by?"

Dev checked the clock. "I don't know. I was napping. I want to, but I am so out of it."

"I hated to say I was feeling the same way. I was hoping I wouldn't disappoint you. I am so fricken sore I just want to lie in bed."

Laughing softly, Dev replied, "Me too, so don't worry about it. Look, my folks want to meet you. Can you come with me to their house tomorrow for a barbeque?"

"Yeah? Meet the parents? I must rate."

"If you don't want to, I understand."

"No. I do. But not on the bike."

"I'll pick you up."

"Why don't you come early so we can fuck first?"

"You're so romantic!" Dev teased.

"No, horny."

"Okay. I'll stop by your place tomorrow at around one? I take it since you work from home you'll be available."

"Yes. Perfect. I can't wait, Dev."

"See ya then, sexy."

"You got it."

Dev hung up and smiled warmly. Yes, Sam was great. This could work out.

chapter Eleven

Motivating himself to get out of bed, Dev made himself a late dinner. By nine he finally had enough energy to go and unpack his bike and bring up his dirty clothing to the condo.

In a pair of gym shorts and a cotton tee, he jogged down the stairs and across the parking lot to his garage, a plastic bag in his hand. Clicking the remote, the door elevated for him as he stood by. He turned on the light and untied the bungee cords that secured his tent and sleeping bag. The daylight had begun fading and since the garage was east of the condo building, the sun had lowered behind it, casting darkness across the pavement. Setting his tent on a wooden shelf, his sleeping bag next to it to bring to the cleaners eventually, Dev began stuffing all the items from his saddlebags into the garbage bag.

The sound of a loud motorcycle drew his attention. Wondering what kind it was, for it sounded like a Harley, Dev finished emptying one of the compartments, moving to the other side.

The noise grew so loud, it echoed in his garage. Raising his head, Dev was surprised to see its bright headlight pull into his parking area and riding his way. He didn't know of another tenant that had a motorcycle and watched to see where it stopped.

As Dev paused to look as the man on the bike came into focus he gasped, "Holy shit!"

The moment Dev recognized him, the man identified Dev as well. The bike roared towards him in an obvious angry gesture. Dev jumped back as the front wheel entered his garage. Tony, in his jeans, muscle T-shirt, and no helmet, shut down the engine and hopped off, appearing homicidal.

Instinctively Dev dropped the bag he was holding and held up his hands in defense.

"You son of a bitch!" Tony roared. "You fucking told my wife I cheated on her!"

"What?" Dev choked in surprise.

Tony grabbed Dev's shirt and shoved him against the cement wall of the garage. "Why? Why did you fuck me up like that?"

"I didn't tell her!"

"If you didn't who did?" Tony's teeth showed in his snarl.

"How the fuck should I know? Maybe she's just bluffing because she knows what an asshole you are." Dev pushed him back, brushing off his arms. "How did you figure out where I live?"

"What are you, stupid? Everyone has a list of club members' addresses."

"I don't."

"Do you have any idea what I have to deal with now? Because of you? She's out of her head with rage." Tony drew closer, menacing.

"Look," Dev shouted, "believe me, though I owe you that for what you did to me at the bar, and I'd gladly admit it if I did, I didn't do it."

Tony shoved Dev with a powerful thrust.

Dev stumbled back for balance. Then to his shock and awe, Tony leapt up, smacked the light bulb with his fist, shattering it and leaving them in darkness. A split second later, Tony trapped Dev against the garage wall.

His heart going wild in his chest, Dev imagined another knee to the groin. As he waited, he could hear Tony's deep raspy breathing. A growl of hatred emerged from Tony. "I should kill you."

Knowing damn well he wouldn't get killed, because the opposite was so apparent, Dev grabbed Tony's jaw and kissed him.

Immediately Tony turned his face aside violently shaking Dev, and knocking him back against the wall. "Don't do that!" Tony snarled in fury. "Don't fucking do that again. You stupid fag!"

Dev heard the last word crack with emotion. Gripping Tony's upper arms, Dev barreled with him across the garage, slamming Tony into the opposite wall. When he had Tony pinned, Dev connected their mouths again.

Tony whimpered in anguish and made another attempt to push Dev back. Dev trapped Tony's wrists and pressed them against the concrete, grinding his hips into Tony's.

Jerking his head to the side, Tony released a sob-like moan. "Get away from me!"

"You came to me. Remember?" Dev panted, pressing his chest against Tony's heaving ribcage.

"God, I hate you!"

"Do you?" Dev humped Tony's body, feeling his large, hard cock.

"Yes. Leave me alone." Tony pushed Dev back.

Catching his breath, Dev stared at him. Tony rubbed his face in agony. When Dev spotted blood, he rushed him, pulling his hands back to look. The swat at the light bulb had gashed Tony's knuckles. "Why did you *really* come here?" Dev hissed.

"She accused me of cheating!" Tony roared.

"I didn't even know if you had. I saw you with women, but I had no clue if you fucked them. So if she heard it, it wasn't from me," Dev enunciated clearly.

"It had to be from you." Tony forced Dev back again. "You're the only one with a personal vendetta. You realize now she'll fuck me up with my job. My family?"

"I swear I didn't call her!"

When Dev reached to touch him again in comfort, Tony reacted violently, whacking Dev back so hard, Dev fell to the concrete floor. Once Tony lunged for him, Dev cringed, waiting for the kicking.

As Tony landed on top of him, Dev flinched and reached up to brace the crushing weight. Tony wrestled with Dev, trapping his arms to the dirty floor. Staring up at Tony in fear, Dev had no idea what the hell he was thinking. Tony appeared to be out of his mind.

The minute Tony released his grip on Dev's hands, moving towards his throat, Dev gasped and tried to twist away. But instead of choking him, Tony's hands held Dev's head tightly.

Pressing Dev into the hard floor painfully, Tony connected to Dev's lips.

On contact Dev was virtually on fire.

That wild man sucked at his tongue and mouth, groaning with so much agony it was painful to hear.

His heart exploding in his chest, Dev needed air but didn't want to pull back from the kiss.

Then as if reality smacked Tony senseless, he stumbled off Dev and to his feet, wiping at his mouth with his bleeding hand.

Shocked to the core, Dev tried to sit up though his body was shaking in spasms of anxiety. When Tony made a move for his Harley, Dev scrambled to his feet. "No! Wait!"

"Leave me alone. Stay away from me! Do you hear me?" Tony was in tears.

"Tony! Calm down before you ride. I'll leave you alone. Just stand here and get your head straight."

"Fuck you! Fuck you faggot!" Tony straddled his bike and it roared and ricocheted noise all around the dark lot.

As he vanished into the night, Dev held onto the seat of his Kawasaki to steady himself. He didn't understand any of this. None of it.

But then again why did it make total sense?

After a long time to recover, staring at the bag of clothing on the floor and regaining his composure, Dev continued with his chore, shaking and upset. The contents of the saddlebags in his grasp, Dev shut off the light in reflex, muttering profanity to himself because it was broken. Closing the garage behind him, he staggered to the lobby. He fought to get the key in the door he was trembling so much. Dragging the sack up one flight of stairs to his door, Dev struggled once again with a key, finally getting inside his home. Dropping the sack, kicking off his shoes, he found a bottle of whiskey in his cupboard and a glass. Filling it, Dev shot it down, wiping his mouth, staring out at the dark sliding glass doors of his deck. As he poured another, he noticed blood on his fingers. Steadying himself, he gulped a second shot, capping the bottle and forcing himself to walk to the bathroom. He turned on the light. Blood was streaked across his cheek. Tony's blood.

Running the tap, Dev splashed his face and hands. Leaning over the basin, water dripping down his skin, Dev convulsed with a sob. Slowly sliding down to the floor, Dev leaned against the bathroom wall and wiped at his eyes when they ran with hot tears.

"What am I doing? I must be out of my mind."

Getting to his feet, Dev knew it was growing late but wasn't thinking of time. He picked up the phone and dialed. "Babe?"

"Dev?"

"Please. Can I come over?"

"Yes, of course. You okay?"

"I just need to hang out with you."

"I'll be waiting."

"Thanks." Dev hung up, scuffed his feet as he gathered his car keys, wallet, and shoes, locked up, and drove his Mustang to Sam's.

~

Sam had been lying in bed watching television in his briefs. Finding a pair of gym shorts, Sam turned on the light in the living room and stood at the front window of his condo to watch for a car. He wanted Dev with him, but something was very wrong. Dev sounded horrible. Sam had no idea what could have happened.

Within fifteen minutes a sports car pulled into a guest spot, the headlights flicking off. Anticipating the buzzer, Sam hit the entry release button and opened his door as he waited.

The sight of Dev looking completely spent unnerved him. Waiting as Dev entered his home, Sam noticed the back of his shirt and shorts were covered in dirt, like he had been in another fight.

"What the hell happened now?"

Dev slapped his keys on a counter, wrapped around Sam and hugged him, his weight dropping on Sam heavily.

Caressing Dev's back in comfort, Sam squeezed him tight. "You want a drink?" When Dev leaned back, Sam caught a scent of alcohol on his breath. "Or did you already have one?"

"Had one."

"Come on. Sit down." Sam gestured to his couch.

As if Dev was reluctant to let him go, he clung to Sam and brought him with him to the sofa. Dev slipped off his shoes, tucking one leg under him as he sat.

"What the hell is going on?" Sam asked, pushing Dev's brown hair back from his forehead.

"Tony."

"Tony?" Sam was shocked. It was the last thing he expected. "You still angry for what he did at Sturgis?"

"You have no idea what he did to me there."

"Don't I?"

"No, Sam, I didn't tell you."

Suspicion reared its ugly head. But thinking rationally, Sam disregarded it. "You going to tell me?"

"Yes. I need to tell you."

"I'm listening."

Dev held both of Sam's hands in his, toying with his fingers nervously. "That day we split up?"

"Yes."

"I was drinking on my own. I didn't know where you were and you didn't answer your cell phone."

Sam nodded, waiting in apprehension.

"Well, Tony found me and began his little torment game."

"Oh, Devlin," Sam sighed, caressing his face again.

"But it got out of hand." Dev licked at his cut lip, continuing, "We fought pretty hard, Sam. I swear it was very violent and

176

angry. Then I began to get the idea he was just deep in the closet."

Sam laughed. "That's absurd."

"Oh? He was hard as a fucking rock from our little tussle."

Recoiling at the comment, Sam asked, "How do you know?"

Dev fidgeted nervously. "Look, Sam, I just want to come clean here. I don't know where you and I stand as far as being in some kind of relationship..."

"Tell me you didn't screw him." Sam didn't realize how crushed he'd feel.

"Hell no. But...we did kiss."

"You and Tony kissed?" Sam narrowed his eyes at him. "Come on, Dev."

"Let me finish." Dev grabbed both Sam's hands again. "Like I was saying, he and I were really roughing each other up, I mean seriously. But that fucker was attracted to me and I think his attraction was killing him and making him even angrier."

Sam never moved his attention from Dev's blue eyes.

"I know this sounds inconceivable, but at one point when I had him pinned to a wall behind a bar, he planted his lips on me. Well, at that moment two giant gay-bashing dickheads spotted it. And what does good old Tony do? He pointed at me and said I was trying to rape him."

Sam choked and blinked his eyes. "Oh, shit. No."

"Yes! I am not kidding," Dev responded. "I freaked. Both these fuckers were massive and covered in tattoos. I thought I was a dead man."

"What did Tony do?"

"He split! He left me with those monsters to fight alone."

Sam released one of Dev's hands and cupped his behind Dev's neck affectionately. "You actually managed to fight off two men?"

"I did. I remembered my dad used to get crazy. I just kept thinking about how he would react in a fight. I played dirty. Very dirty."

"You had no choice. Oh, Devlin, this is killing me."

"I should have just told you, but I kept thinking you and I weren't going to amount to much. All that pushing away you kept doing, well, I don't want to get into it again."

"No. I'm glad you told me."

"There's more."

Sam stroked the back of Dev's neck lovingly. "I'm listening."

"Just now. Tonight. I was clearing out the saddlebags in my garage. Tony showed up."

Sam dropped his hand to his lap. "What?"

Nodding to emphasize it, Dev went on. "He was out of his head, Sam. He pulled into my garage with his Harley and accused me of telling his wife he cheated on her at Sturgis."

"Did you?"

"No!" Dev glared at him.

"So you fought again?"

"Yes. Again. But it was different this time. It was like the whole thing was some macho act, and the real reason he had come was to figure out if he was attracted to a man. To me."

"What did you do?"

"It was almost the same thing as at Buffalo Chip. We fought really violently. Me slamming him into the wall, him slamming me. That fucker punched the light bulb in my ceiling and smashed it, cutting his knuckles good."

Sam cringed.

"Then it was back to the same stupid game with him. He pushes me back and then acts like he wants it."

A cold sensation washed into Sam's gut. "It's you who wants him."

178

Dev's eyes grew pale. "I can't. He's insane."

"But you're attracted to him."

Welling up, Dev admitted, "Yes. A little."

"And you thought it was a good idea to come here and tell me?" Sam pushed Dev's hands off his lap.

"Sam! I don't want anything to do with him. Look at me." Dev held out his arms. "I'm a punching bag and covered in bruises from associating with him. I'll bet you a hundred bucks he and his wife pound each other. I want nothing to do with him."

"But? And?" Sam rose up, glowering down at him.

Standing to meet him face to face, Dev grabbed Sam's shoulders. "What you did on the way home, in Toledo, that clinched it for me."

"What the fuck are you talking about?"

"Sam, you showed me what you were really about. That whole trip during Sturgis, the wimp act, I was so turned off I couldn't imagine seeing you seriously. But I caught a glimpse of the real you at that moment when you kissed me."

Sam was boiling mad. "You? All this is suddenly your decision? You're the one to decide if we're a couple based on *my* actions? Are you kidding me?"

"Yes! No! Oh, God, I'm fucking it up." Dev moaned.

"Listen to yourself, Dev. You come over here in a state after battling with a straight, handsome, Italian stud, kissing him, figuring out he's got a hard-on for you? And now you tell me I'm the one you want, like I have no say? I'm not the wimp you think I am, Devlin."

Dev gripped Sam's upper arms. "Don't do this to me."

"Do what to you?" Sam shoved him back.

"Don't reject me for being honest!"

"Fuck you! You can't tell me how to feel."

"I knew it! I knew you couldn't handle it. That's why I didn't tell you what really happened at Buffalo!"

"You asshole. You didn't tell me because you fucking cheated on me!"

Dev pushed Sam back. "Cheated? One fucking peck?"

"Don't get physical with me." Sam used one hand to straight arm Dev back.

A look of fury raced over Dev's face. As Dev lunged for Sam, Sam braced himself for the impact. His back connected to the plasterboard wall with a slap. Instantly, Dev's mouth was sucking at his.

At the contact, Sam's brain went haywire. He wrapped his arms around Dev's neck, leapt up to straddle his hips and locked his legs around Dev's waist.

Dev tightened his hold on Sam, humping up against Sam's crotch where he stood.

Cupping Dev's face, Sam ate at his mouth, tasting blood seeping from his cut lip at their ferocity of their kissing.

An animal-like snarl rumbled from Dev. Sam felt his skin prickle with fire. He was so turned on by Dev, even Dev's sideways glance could flip his switch. Now? With them about to begin a frenzied sexual bout? Sam was in heat, in lust, and unfortunately, in love.

Sliding his legs down Dev's body, Sam found the floor with his feet and started forcing Dev into his bedroom. *You want a fight? I'll fucking fight!*

Like two wildcats, Dev and Sam growled, gripping biceps with iron grasps, thrusting their hips to connect with violently hot pelvis strikes.

Shoving Dev back, Sam tore at Dev's shirt fiercely revealing his scratched skin. Ripping it over Dev's head, Sam dug his fingers into Dev's shorts and wrenched them off his legs,

180

smacking the material against a wall like cracking a whip. Sam stood over Dev as he lay back, naked, panting, staring up at him with anticipation. Reaching for his nightstand, Sam dug in a drawer and located a rubber. His breath heaving, Dev licked his cracked lip and waited.

Sam slipped off his shorts and briefs, rolling the condom on his dick, which was as stiff as a mast at the moment.

His eyes never leaving Sam's, Dev bent his knees and opened to a wide straddle.

Once Sam had the tube of lube in his hand, he crawled between Dev's legs. Admiring the view of Dev open, passive, and exposed, Sam's lip curled in a wicked grin.

Squeezing out a blob on his fingers, Sam pressed Dev's thighs farther apart forcefully, and knelt between them. "Who the fuck do you think you are, Dev? Huh?" Sam taunted. "You think you control me?"

Gliding two fingers into Dev's ass, Sam watched Dev's face as he massaged his prostate from inside.

"Oh, God..." Dev's cock bobbed, he arched his back, and hissed through a clenched jaw.

Grinning at the sight of Dev acting the perfect submissive, Sam removed his hand, wanting Dev to go insane with his yearning. As he predicted Dev's breathing was like a race horse blowing. "More."

Setting the tips of his fingers against Dev's ass, Sam waited. Dev bucked his hips, trying to get him in. "Sam...please."

Smiling in pleasure, Sam pushed three digits in, deep and slow.

"*Oh, God...*" Dev whimpered, clenched his jaw and eyes as he pumped his hips up and reached for his own cock.

Sam slapped his hand away from it with a vicious, stinging whack.

As if he needed to do everything in his power to resist masturbating, Dev trapped his own arms behind his back, causing his pelvis to rise up higher.

Sam pulled out. Waiting.

Dev moaned like he was in pain. "Again…Sam."

Another drop of lube, and four fingers were in, massaging that magic spot, slowly, yet deeply. Sam was so hot his cock was throbbing like his pulse and harder than he could ever remember it getting.

"*Augh! Sam! Ahh…*" Dev's veins were showing in his neck, his chest had contracted and tightened to two high round mounds, the nipples standing erect.

Moving his slick fingers in and out, rubbing against Dev's prostate in leisurely strokes, Sam began inching his body closer.

"*Oh, God…oh, God…*touch my cock…touch my cock." Dev sounded like he was begging. *Good. Beg me.*

Sam removed his hand, watching Dev's face.

When his eyes blinked open and those blue orbs lit up, Dev gasped, "Don't stop!"

"Fuck you," Sam purred.

"Yes! Fuck me!" Dev pleaded, his hips rising in desire. "Sam, take it. Goddamn it! Fuck me hard."

Sam pushed two fingers back inside, causing Dev to swear profanely and let out a sob-like moan. "Nice?"

"Oh, Christ…" Dev swallowed loudly. "Do you have any idea what you're doing to me?" When Sam removed his fingers again, Dev whined in agony.

Chuckling wickedly, Sam leaned over Dev's body, placing his cock on Dev's well oiled anus. "Oh, yes. I do, Dev. I do." Pushing the tip in, Sam paused.

"More."

Sam entered deeper.

"More!" Dev roared.

Letting out a guttural growl, Sam thrust hard against Dev's body, penetrating to the base of his cock.

Dev's hands flew out from behind his back to grab his own dick. Sam trapped them and pinned them to the bed.

With Dev going berserk under him, pumping his hips against Sam to get deeper still, Sam pulled out to the tip, plunging back inside again to the root.

"Please...ahh...Sam..."

"Fuck you, cocksucker." Sam snarled, "Who you calling a wimp now?"

"Me! I'm the wimp!" Dev gasped, trying to free his hands.

"You're the fucking woman in this relationship, Young, never forget that."

"Oh, God..." Dev pushed his hips up to meet Sam's pelvis.

Sam drew his cock all the way out, rushing it back in to the base. Dev's fingers were clenching and unclenching, the veins in his forearms were like velvet ropes standing out from his tanned skin. Writhing under him, Dev tried to free one of his hands. Sam could only chuckle at the attempt.

When Dev finally opened his eyes, and the expression of hunger filled his face, Sam thrust in again, this time, continuing with fast hard pumps. Dev bucked to get his hands free. Sam knew damn well he wanted them on this cock. Watching this muscular god thrashing under him, the incredible passion and beauty of Dev, his scent, his shuddering moans, Sam felt it rushing up his spine. Christ how he adored this man. It was too much a fantasy, too hot to screw him this way. But it was what he had wanted to do from the first day they had met in the bar in Kettering. He wanted it on his terms, his way. Not hiding in some miniscule tent in a homophobic campground.

The shivering lightning bolt of energy that rushed to his cock, the sensation of his sperm bursting through the tip of his dick, Sam's body quivered in pleasure as he came. Shutting his eyelids tight, he grunted in a low, throaty gasp. Plunging inside Dev's body, deeper than he had been previously, Sam's cock shivered in the heat and the orgasm was mind blowing in its intensity and duration.

As he gulped the air, Sam opened his eyes. Dev was staring at him in awe, silently pleading. Sitting back gradually, the head of his cock still inside Dev, Sam released Dev's hands. Instantly they raced to his own dick. Sam slapped Dev's fingers to discourage him.

Flinching back, Dev laid his palms flat on the bed obediently.

Sam pulled out. Recuperating, he kept his eyes on Dev. Gently Sam removed the condom, dropping it over the side of the bed.

"Thanks, Dev. But I think it's time you went home."

"What?" Dev choked in shock.

Sam loved the reaction. "Oh? You think I want to please you? After what you told me tonight?"

Dev made a noise of frustration and went back to trying to jerk off.

Sam gripped Dev's wrists and lunged over his body, pinning his arms to the bed by his head. "You don't know me at all, Devlin Young."

"I'm beginning to figure that out." Dev's lip curled into a wicked smile.

"You get the idea I was some lightweight? Easy to push around?"

"Yes." Dev laughed.

"Just because I didn't want to get a fat lip and cut over my eye?" Sam licked Dev's split lip.

"Yes!" Dev chuckled again, rubbing his erection against Sam's body.

"That just makes me smarter than you, asshole."

"I'm beginning to see that now."

"You don't know shit, Devlin. You think you do, but you don't."

"God! I need to fucking come! Stop tormenting me!"

Sam released Dev's wrists, grabbed the sides of his face and drew him up to his mouth. As Sam fucked him with his tongue, Dev clamped his legs around Sam's body and rode him.

Taking a handful of Dev's hair in each fist, Sam pulled back from the kiss and gazed at him. Running his tongue over the stubble on Dev's jaw, Sam licked him from his chin to his neck. Dev moaned and pumped his hips hard against Sam, as if craving and not getting enough friction.

Sam ran his teeth along the tight salty skin of Dev's neck, sucking hard.

"Don't give me a hickey, you mother fucker!"

Grinning wickedly, Sam did just that. Sucking Dev's tight hard throat into his mouth, until he was certain it was red. When he was good and ready, Sam released the suction and ran his tongue down Dev's sternum.

While Dev whimpered in agony, Sam made his way to Dev's nipple. Lapping at it, sucking and nipping it, Sam had Dev going mad under him. While pressing Dev's biceps into the mattress, Sam continued his tongue tickling downward. Long wet licks ran from Dev's sides to his hips. Releasing the hold he had on Dev's arms, Sam gripped his inner thighs and pressed them apart roughly. With Dev's genitals exposed, Sam began gnawing on his balls.

"Oh, God! I can't take this anymore!" Dev cried.

"Shut up, wimp." Sam slapped Dev's hand back as it sought to grasp his cock.

Using his face to caress the smooth skin of Dev's cock, Sam felt the dewy drops oozing from the slit drag along his cheek. With the tip of his tongue, Sam lapped at it.

A deep painful howl of longing echoed off the bedroom walls. Sam loved it.

Clamping both hands on the base of Dev's cock, Sam teased the head with his lips and tongue.

"Oh, God, oh, God!" Dev growled. "I'm in pain! Let me come!"

"Fuck you." Sam slid the head of Dev's dick in and out of his mouth quickly. Dev's hips jerked up every chance he got to deepen the penetration. Sam stopped and stared at Dev's cock as it bobbed, blushing red, slick with saliva.

"Sam... Oh, God..."

Sam closed his eyes and glided Dev's cock all the way into his mouth to the root. He could hear Dev almost weep with relief. Holding him still while his tongue drew patterns over the underside of his penis, Sam very slowly penetrated Dev with one finger, back inside the slick passage.

As he massaged that magic spot, Sam withdrew his mouth quickly, causing Dev's cock to stand straight up from his body.

Dev cried in agony, hovering his hands in the air wanting to grip his own cock and knowing he would get slapped for it. Dev's hips raised and his entire body shuddered in a chill.

Rubbing his finger inside that well-oiled opening, making Dev writhe in longing, Sam smiled wickedly. "Beg me, cocksucker."

"Please..."

"Please what?"

"Please make me come."

"Who's the master in this relationship?"

"You are, Sam, you are."

"Damn fucking right." Smiling, Sam lowered his mouth and allowed that stiff cock to enter him again. He pulled at it with hard suction and sluggishly drew Dev's cock out of his mouth. Just as he was deepening his next wet suck, Dev's cock went rigid.

It was as if his body was connected to an electric wire. Dev's entire length tightened, his back arched and his head jerked back. A deep vibrating moan followed by a choking gasp preceded the shot of semen. It hit Sam's mouth with so much force he was unprepared for it. Swallowing him down, Sam kept his lips moving on Dev's shaft feeling the aftershocks still rumble through his organ.

Removing his finger, Sam knelt up, sweat dripping down both of them, and stared at Dev's expression.

~

Never in Dev's wildest fantasies did he ever imagine sex like this. Tony? Who the hell was Tony?

"Holy Christ..." Dev cried.

"You alive?"

"Barely..." Dev wiped at his dewy face.

Sam crawled up his body to rest on top of him.

Seeing his wicked, knowing smile, Dev started to laugh though he was spent. "Holy shit."

"Satisfied, Devlin?"

"Don't look so fucking smug," Dev laughed. "I'm still waiting for you to send me home so no one finds out."

"No. Not this time." Sam coiled around him.

"Jesus, where did you learn to have sex like that? I'm speechless."

"Good. Because most of the talk you come out with is shit."

"Shut up!" Dev laughed, putting Sam in a headlock.

"We should wash up, and go to sleep."

When Sam stood, reaching back, Dev could barely move. Taking his outstretched hand, Dev made it to his feet.

Feeling like a walking zombie, Dev managed to wash up enough for his satisfaction, only to stumble back to bed.

Once Sam had made sure all the lights were out, and the door was locked, he joined Dev under the blankets.

"Good night, Dev."

"Night, Sam, you hot mother-fucker who I will never let go of."

A soft chuckle came out of Sam.

Dev wrapped around him, pulling him close, and fell asleep nestled in Sam's hair.

Chapter Twelve

When Dev opened his eyes he felt slightly disoriented. It had been almost a week since he slept in his own bed. Hearing deep breathing, Dev rolled to his side and found Sam.

This beautiful twenty-eight-year-old spitfire with the chocolate colored eyes and hair was sprawled out against the crisp white sheets like a Greek deity. His naked, darkly tanned torso and legs revealed, the sheet twisted only around his upper thighs, that fantastic white ass exposed, Dev went into heat. His morning hard-on throbbed as he admired Sam.

Oh you fantastic fucker!

Lithe, long, tight, and firm, from his cut chest to his rolling runner's calves, Dev felt as if he was seeing Sam for the first time. *Last night! Christ, last night!*

Gripping his own cock, Dev pumped it a few times and felt like jerking off all over him.

I'm insane! Look at this man! Remember the sex last night?

Dev couldn't imagine being with anyone else. No way. Not now.

Bending one knee, using it to prop him up on his side while he masturbated, Dev kept racing his eyes from Sam's long brown hair to his muscular shoulders and arms, down his back to his tight ass.

"Oh fuck it." Dev hopped on top of Sam's back, pushing his cock between Sam's ass crack.

Waking up with a start, Sam twisted around to see what Dev was doing.

"Augh!" Dev groaned in frustration at not getting enough friction, leaned up and grabbed the lube.

"Jesus, Dev!"

Fumbling with a rubber, Dev almost didn't use it, but managed to roll it on, squeezed a splotch of gel into his hand and prepped quickly.

"Can I wake up first?" Sam laughed at the absurdity.

"No!" Dev elevated Sam's hips and pushed in.

"Ah!"

"Fuck you!" Dev wrapped around him. "You torture me, I'll torture you."

"It doesn't hurt! The lube is just cold."

Pressing his face against Sam's body to stifle his laughter, Dev moved in a rhythm and felt more at ease with his dick inside Sam. "Better...*ohh*..." Searching around Sam's hips, Dev bumped into Sam's erection and wrapped his fingers tightly around it. "Last night, Sam...oh, my God, last night..." Dev crooned, thrusting in and pumping Sam's cock at the same time.

"Oh, yes, that's it." Sam arched his back in delight.

"You..." Dev plunged in with each word. "Hot. Mother. Fucker."

"Ah!" Sam shot out come into Dev's fingers.

Closing his eyes, Dev pressed his hips tight against Sam's ass and climaxed. Fingering Sam's sticky cock gently, loving the way it felt and imaging what it looked like covered in creamy sperm, Dev let out a deep satisfied moan.

Finally pulling out, rolling off of Sam, Dev removed the condom and dropped it on the floor.

"Well!" Sam laughed. "Good morning!"

Giving Sam a seductive glare, Dev licked the sperm off his fingers.

Laughing wickedly, Sam wrapped around him, wriggling all over Dev's hot skin. "Oh, I so can get used to this."

"Me too. You have no idea." Dev cuddled Sam closer.

Leaning back, Sam rubbed noses with Dev playfully. "Let's not get out of bed."

"We don't have to until later."

"Good." Sam ran light kisses all over Dev's forehead and cheeks.

"I can't believe the change in you."

Pausing, Sam gave Dev a pained look. "Do we have to keep rehashing?"

"No. Sorry. It's just that, well, if you were like this at Sturgis…"

Pressing his hips harder against Dev's, Sam asked wryly, "Yeah? Then what?"

"I'd have proposed by now." Dev gave him a wicked smile. "I feel like handing you a diamond ring from my bended knee. Anything to keep you with me."

"I kept trying to convince you."

"You have now!" Dev laughed in amazement.

"What are you going to do about Tony?"

"Tony who?"

That lit Sam up. "Good thinking. Gee, Devlin, maybe there is a brain at this end of you after all." Sam tapped Dev's head.

"Ha ha."

"Let me take a piss and brush my teeth, then we'll get back to some more sex."

"Good idea," Dev replied enthusiastically.

~

Once they had freshened up, Sam rested his head on Dev's chest and stroked the light line of fur that dissected Dev's lower abdomen to his dark curly pubes.

Dev was running his fingers lazily through Sam's hair. Sam knew it would be this wonderful when they had the chance to unwind and be themselves. He was surprised it was so hard to convince Dev of that, but at least he felt he finally had. Mulling over the rest of the afternoon and their meeting with Mr. and Mrs. Young, Sam asked softly, "What do you think your parents will think of me?"

"They'll love you." Dev dug into Sam's thick mane, combing through it.

"Yeah?"

"Yeah. Especially Mom."

"I can't imagine having a dad cool enough to have ridden to Sturgis."

"You kidding me? My parents were hippies during that whole Haight-Ashbury thing."

"That is so cool." Sam smiled cupping his hand over Dev's soft genitals.

"They're almost too cool. They're real hold-outs from that whole drop-out, tune-in, turn-on mentality. I think they still sneak a joint now and then. But never when I'm around."

"You have any siblings?"

"Nope. Just me."

"My parents are the exact opposite."

"Really?"

"Yes. Dad's ex-army, mom's ex-air force."

"I take it that's what influenced your brother."

"Yes. Rusty wanted to be in uniform since he was three." Sam laughed softly.

"Not you?"

"No. I suppose I was more the computer geek."

"Yeah, right," Dev replied sarcastically.

Sitting up so he could see his face, Sam added, "I was. Totally."

"You just don't seem like that. I can't picture it."

"Like I said. You don't know me at all, Mr. Young."

"I feel like I know you much better now."

"Good. To be honest, Dev, I didn't really think anything like this would happen during that rally. I never even assumed I'd meet a gay man at the club."

"Me neither."

"Well, and if you weren't there, I suppose I would have hung out with Doug and Ralph."

"And Tony."

Seeing Dev's impish grin, Sam nodded. "Probably. It would have been a very different experience."

"It would have been worse. If you weren't with me, you know, having some fun, I think I would have really resented going."

"That bad?"

"Yes. I had some euphoric recall of the place. I suppose when I was a young teen, women still turned me on a little. I wasn't really mentally prepared to think otherwise."

"Not me. I've known I liked men since I became sexual."

"You're lucky. It saved you from making the mistakes I've made."

"Do you regret your marriage?"

193

"Yes. In some ways it set me back. And I'm not talking money. I mean, time-wise. Here I am, thirty, and I'm just now getting into my homosexual prime. I feel like a late-bloomer."

"Do you feel the need to play around more?"

Dev dragged Sam on top of him. "Not now."

"Later?"

"Shut up and kiss me."

Sam leaned down to his lips. Dev coiled his arms and legs around him and hummed in pleasure. When Sam parted to look at Dev, he whispered, "I've found what I was looking for."

"You sure? You haven't known me for very long. I'm slightly mental."

"Who isn't?"

"I hope I don't disappoint you."

"I hope so too." Sam pulled him into a passionate kiss.

~

By one Dev had driven them back to his place so he could change his clothes.

As he pulled his Mustang into a space in the lot, he choked in surprise.

Sam gasped, "He's waiting for you?"

"I don't believe this." Dev turned off the ignition and they climbed out.

Assertively Sam grabbed Dev by the hand as they made their way to Tony who was sitting on his bike in front of Dev's garage.

When Tony noticed Sam, he seemed to go pale.

"What do you want?" Dev asked. "More accusations?"

Sam wrapped around Dev's waist, holding on for dear life as if Dev would race to Tony's arms.

"What's he doing here?" Tony tilted his chin to Sam.

"He's my partner." Dev clung to Sam, holding onto his shoulder.

Addressing Sam, Tony said, "You know your so-called partner tried to seduce me."

"I know all about it, Tony." Sam rubbed Dev's chest, being as obvious about this possession as he could. "Why don't you just find someone else to bother? Haven't you done enough to him?"

"Me? He's the one who kissed me and groped my balls."

"Get lost," Dev fumed.

"Yeah, well, I was coming to say goodbye anyway." Tony stuck his key into the Harley's ignition.

"Leaving town?" Sam asked.

"Yes, as a matter of fact." Tony paused before starting it.

"Come by for some make-up sex?" Dev taunted.

"You wish." Tony shook his head but he wasn't fooling anyone.

"Goodbye!" Sam waved in exaggeration.

Feeling badly, Dev broke his and Sam's embrace and reached out his hand. "Good luck to you, Tony."

Appearing surprised at the kindness, Tony took Dev's hand. "Thanks, Dev."

"I hope you find what you're looking for."

Tony's eyes darted back at Sam and he whispered, "I thought I had."

"Sorry, babe." Dev winked.

When Tony kissed Dev's knuckles, Dev twisted back to see Sam was about to explode. Taking his hand back gently, Dev reached back for his true lover.

Sam fell quickly in at his side.

A wry smile found Tony's mouth. "Sam, you are one lucky fucker."

"Ha! That's rich coming from a homophobe like you." Sam snorted.

"You're right. It is." He started the engine and the Harley roared to life.

Seeing Tony's lingering gaze, Dev waved to him again.

He returned it, leaving the lot in silence when the echoing noise finally died back.

Feeling slightly let down, as he stared after him, Dev felt Sam poke his side.

"Hm?"

"Stop fantasizing."

"Why? Is that a crime?" Dev directed them back to the front lobby door.

"It is if it's about Tony!"

Dev laughed softly as he found his key. Opening the door, and turning back to Sam's pout, Dev dragged him into the lobby and swung him in his arms for a kiss.

Dipping him in a passionate swoon, Dev set him back on his feet again and ascended the stairs.

"Wow!" Sam followed eagerly.

"Still worried?"

"No!"

"Good." Dev smiled happily.

The minute Dev opened the door to his condo, Sam was attached to his lips, digging his hands into Dev's shorts.

Breaking up with laughter as he tried to close his door, Dev asked, "Still horny? After all the sex we just had?"

"Seeing Tony got me hot."

"What?" Dev gasped in surprise.

"Imagining you two muscular studs battling and then butt-fucking? That's like a fantasy right out of your books."

"How do you know? You've never read any of my books, Samuel." Dev rocked him side to side in his arms.

"Samuel? You think I can't imagine what you write, *Devlin*?" Sam shook his head in disbelief.

Dev picked Sam up so Sam could wrap his legs around his hips. "I'd fuck you right now if we didn't have to go to my folks' place."

"Tell them we'll be late." Sam rubbed his hard cock against Dev's.

"We already are. Let me change." Dev set Sam on his feet.

Dev dug out a fresh pair of briefs and jeans. When he spun around to toss them on the bed to strip, Sam was standing in his doorway with his hard cock hanging out of his jeans.

Shivering at the sight, Dev dropped down in front of him instantly and opened his mouth. Holding Sam's ass tight, Dev slid him in and out of his throat. Sam dug his hands through Dev's hair and arched his back, thrusting his hips deeper into Dev's mouth.

Dev held the base of Sam's cock and quickened his pace. A hiss of air was released from Sam's lips and he climaxed.

Dev moaned and swallowed him down, sucking the last drop out on his tongue.

Setting back, wiping Sam's dick off with his hand to dry it, Dev stood up and announced, "Now can I change?"

"Yes. Go on."

"Thank you." Dev gave Sam a wicked smile.

~

Parking in the long double driveway in Beavercreek, Dev shut the car motor and climbed out. Waiting for Sam by the pathway to the front door, Dev held out his hand.

"You ready for this?" Dev asked.

"Yup."

Dev rang the bell and tried the door. It was unlocked. "Hello?"

"Devlin!" Jan hurried to greet them.

Dev hugged him. "Dad, this is Sam."

"Hello, Sam. Nice to meet you. Pretty one, Dev." Jan shook Sam's hand.

"Baby?"

"Hello, Mom," Dev shouted to her as she rushed in from another room.

She stopped short and gave Sam a good once over. "Wow! Oh, he so much prettier than Carol!"

"Mother!" Dev chided. "Sam, that's my mother, Melinda."

"Get over here good looking!" She opened her arms to him.

Sam chuckled and reached for her hug.

"Mm, he smells delicious. You guys just have sex?"

"Mother! Behave!" Dev laughed in embarrassment.

Seeing Sam was blushing bright from all the attention, Dev reached for his hand. "I tried to warn you."

"No. Don't. I'm very flattered."

Melinda stood in front of Dev and pulled back his shirt. "A hickey! Oh, I love hickeys. Jan, when was the last time you gave me one?"

"Jesus, Ma," Dev choked in humiliation.

"Come on." Melinda gripped Sam's free hand. "Drinks are already on the patio."

Jan gestured for the men to go first behind Melinda.

Walking through the kitchen to the outside deck complete with metal chairs and table, Sam and Dev relaxed as Melinda poured them sangria from a sweating pitcher.

After she set it down, she held Dev's face for closer inspection. "Who did you fight?" She ran her finger over his cracked lip and eyebrow.

198

"A homophobe." Dev nudged her away.

"I warned you." Jan pointed his finger.

Sam added, "A homophobe who was hot for his ass."

"That's normally what they are," Melinda replied, sitting down at the round table for four.

"So? Other than the battle, how was it?" Jan asked.

"Worse than I remembered." Dev sipped his drink.

"How about for you, Sam?"

"Better than I thought it would be." He grinned at Dev.

"Aren't they the cutest couple, Jan?" Melinda gushed. "I told Dev all along I'd rather have a son-in-law than a daughter-in-law. But he had to figure it out for himself."

"Come on, Mom." Dev rolled his eyes.

"Let me get my camera. I want pictures of the two of you." She set her drink down and raced into the house.

"I took some shots on the digital at Sturgis," Dev shouted to her, but she was already gone.

"Email them to us."

"Okay, Dad."

"I hope you know what you're getting into, Sam." Jan refilled all their glasses as Melinda returned with her digital camera.

"I think I can handle him."

"Smile!"

Dev wrapped his arm around Sam.

The flash went off. Melinda checked it out. "Look how cute they are." She showed her husband. "Maybe Sam will let me paint him in the nude."

"Ma!" Dev yelled. "Dad, control her."

Sam was trying not to fall off the chair from his laughter. "You guys are great."

"Sorry, Devlin, that's your mother." Jan shrugged.

Dev wrapped his arms around Sam, "You forgive me for being neurotic now?"

"Yes, dear."

Dev rested his head on Sam's temple.

"Aren't they adorable?"

Dev pecked Sam on the cheek and looked back at his mother who had the camera aimed their way.

"And you thought I was bad?" Dev sighed.

"Will you relax?" Sam ruffed up Dev's hair playfully.

"You tell him, Sam. Dev's too high strung." Melinda set the camera down and sipped her drink.

"I'll try my best." Sam's cheeks were still blushing.

"Let's get the appetizers, Jan." Melinda popped back to her feet again, her muslin skirt whooshing as she ran.

"I'll be right back, boys."

After Jan left, Dev faced Sam. "Thanks for putting up with all this."

"Are you kidding? I'd do anything for you."

"Yeah?"

"Yeah." Sam kissed him and met his eyes. "I adore you, Devlin."

"Wow. That's almost an I love you."

"Almost." Sam smiled.

"Get over here, you sexy leather biker." Dev dragged him off his chair to his lap. As they kissed, Dev heard his mom shouting, "Aren't they adorable?"

Chuckling, Dev deepened the kiss. "I adore you too, Sam."

"Maybe one day soon that will turn into an I love you."

"Maybe." Dev sat back to see Sam's brown eyes and smiled.

The End

About the Author:

Award-winning author G.A. Hauser was born in Fair Lawn, New Jersey, USA and attended university in New York City. She moved to Seattle, Washington where she worked as a patrol officer with the Seattle Police Department. In early 2000 G.A. moved to Hertfordshire, England where she began her writing in earnest and published her first book, In the Shadow of Alexander. Now a full-time writer, G.A. has written over fifty novels, including several best-sellers of gay fiction and is an Honorary Board Member of Gay American Heroes for her support of the foundation. For more information on other books by G.A., visit the author at her official website. www.authorgahauser.com

Awards:

All Romance eBook- Best Author 2009, 2008 and 2007

All Romance eBook- Best novel 2007 *Secrets and Misdemeanors*

All Romance eBook- Best novel 2008 *Mile High*

Other works by G.A. Hauser:

When Adam Met Jack

Attorney Jack Larsen may not have everything he wants, but between his successful career and best friend Mark Richfield, he's content. But when Mark comes out of the closet only to declare his love for ex-LAPD officer Steve Miller, Jack is devastated. Months later and still wounded, he's not looking to be swept off his feet, but it's hard to say no to handsome Hollywood hotshot Adam Lewis.

Adam Lewis has made a name for himself representing some of today's brightest stars. But when his business partner is accused of unethical behavior, he finds himself in need of legal advice. When Adam walks into the law office of Jack Larsen, it's strictly business until he sets eyes on the powerful and sexy hero that's about to rescue his reputation.

When Adam Met Jack is an amazing new novel by Amazon best selling gay fiction author G.A. Hauser featuring characters from Love you Loveday, For Love and Money, and Capital Games. It's got the glamour of the entertainment industry, the drama of the courtroom, and the amazing passion that you've come to expect from every G.A. Hauser book.

Love you, Loveday

Angel Loveday thought he had put his life as a gay soft-porn star of the 1980s behind him. For seventeen years he's hidden his sexuality and sordid past from his teenage son. But when someone threatens Angel's secret and Detective Billy Sharpe is assigned to his case, he finds himself having to once again face them both.

Since his youth Billy Sharpe has had erotic on-screen images of Angel Loveday emblazoned in his mind. Now Angel is there in the flesh, needing his protection and stirring up the passionate fantasies that Billy thought he'd long ago abandoned.

As the harassment continues and the danger grows, Billy and Angel become closer. What began as an instant attraction turns into an undeniable hunger that unlocks Angel's heart. It's a race against time as Billy tries to save the man of his dreams from a life without love and the maniacal stalker hell-bent on destroying him.

To Have and to Hostage

When he was taken hostage by a strange man Michael never expected he'd lose his heart...

Michael Vernon is a rich, spoiled brat with a string of meaningless lovers and an entourage of superficial friends. With no direction in life, he wastes his days spending his father's money and drowning himself in liquor...until he crashes into a man even more desperate than himself, Jarrod Hunter.

Jarrod Hunter grew up on the wrong side of the tracks. Out of work, about to be evicted, and unable to afford his next meal, Jarrod thought he'd reached the end of his rope and was determined to take his life. Then fate intervened delivering him Michael Vernon. Why not take him home, tie him up, and hold him hostage to get the money he needs?

Two men from two different worlds...one dangerous game. Trapped together in close quarters, Jarrod and Michael find themselves sharing their deepest thoughts and fighting an undeniable attraction for each other. As the hours tick by, the captor becomes captivated by his victim and the victim begins to bond with his abductor. This wake up call might prove to be just what Michael needs to set himself free. To Have and to Hostage…sometimes you have to hit bottom before realizing that what you need is standing right in front of you.

Giving Up The Ghost

The visit from beyond the grave that changed their lives forever…

Artist Ryan Monroe had everything he wanted and then in a blink of an eye, he lost what mattered most of all, his soul-mate, Victor. Tortured by an overwhelming sense of grief and unable to move on, his pain spills out, reflected in the blood red hues of his paintings.

Paul Goldman thought he'd found the love of his life in Evan, his beloved pianist. Their mutual passion for music was outweighed only by their passion for one another. They were planning a life-time together, but then one fateful night Evan's was taken. Drowning in sorrow, unable to find solace, the heart-broken violinist has resigned himself to a life alone.

Now it's two years later and something, someone, is bringing them together. Two men, two loves, two great losses…and one hot ghost. Giving up the Ghost by G.A. Hauser, you won't be able to put down!

Capital Games

Let the games begin…

Former Los Angeles Police officer Steve Miller has gone from walking a beat in the City of Angels to joining the rat race as an advertising executive. He knows how cut-throat the industry can be, so when his boss tells him that he's in direct competition with a newcomer from across the pond for a coveted account he's not surprised…then he meets Mark Richfield.

Born with a silver spoon in his mouth and fashion-model good looks, Mark is used to getting what he wants. About to be married, Mark has just nailed the job of his dreams. If the determined Brit could just steal the firm's biggest account right out from under Steve Miller, his life would be perfect.

When their boss sends them together to the Arizona desert for a team-building retreat the tension between the two dynamic men escalates until in the heat of the moment their uncontrollable passion leads them to a sexual experience that neither can forget.

Will Mark deny his feelings and follow through with marriage to a women he no longer wants, or will he realize in time that in the game of love, sometimes you have to let go and lose yourself in order to *really* win.

Secrets and Misdemeanors

When having to hide your love is a crime…

After losing his wife to his best friend and former law partner, David Thornton couldn't imagine finding love again. With his divorce behind him, he wanted only to focus on his job and two children. But then something happened, making David realize that despite believing he had everything he needed, there was someone he desperately wanted—Lyle Wilson.

Young and determined, Lyle arrived in Los Angeles without a penny in his pocket. Before long, however, the sexy construction worker nailed a job remodeling the old office building that held the prestigious Thornton Law Firm. Little did Lyle realize when he gazed upon the handsome and successful David Thornton for the first time that a door would be opened that neither man could close.

Will the two men succumb to the tangled web of societal pressures placed before them, hiding who they are and whom they love? Or will they reveal the truth and set themselves free?

Naked Dragon

Police Officer Dave Harris has just been assigned to one of the worst serial murder cases in Seattle history: The Dragon is hunting young Asian men. In order to solve the crime it's going to take a bit more than good old-fashioned police work. It's going to take handsome FBI Agent Robbie Taylor.

Robbie is an experienced Federal Agent with psychic abilities that allow him to enter the minds of others. You can't hide your secrets and desires from someone that knows your every thought. Some think what Robbie has is a gift, others a skill, but when the mind you have to enter is that of a madman it can also be a curse.

As the corpses pile up and the tension mounts, so does the sexual attraction between the two men. Then a moment of passion leads to a secret affair. Will their love be the distraction that costs them the case and possibly even their lives? Or will the bond forged between them be the key to their survival?

The Kiss

Twenty-five year old actor Scott Epstein is no stranger to the modeling industry. He's done it himself between acting jobs. So when his sister, Claire, casts him in a chewing-gum commercial with the famous British model, Ian Sullivan, he doesn't ask any questions. He's a professional. He'll show up, hit his mark, say his lines, and collect his paycheck. Right?

Ian Sullivan is used to making heads turn. Stunningly handsome, he's accustomed to provocative photo shoots where sex sells everything from perfume to laundry soap. Ian was thrilled when Claire Epstein cast him in the new Minty gum commercial. He has to kiss his co-star on screen? No problem. Until he finds out Scott is the one he has to kiss!

Never before has a commercial featured two men, kissing on screen. Claire knows that the advertisement will be ground-breaking, and Scott knows that his sister needs his performance to be perfect. As the filming progresses and the media circus begins around the controversial advertisement, the chemistry between Ian and Scott heats up and the two men quite simply burn up the screen. Is it all an act? Or, have Ian and Scott entered into a clandestine affair that will lead them to love?

For Love and Money

Handsome Dr. Jason Philips, the heir to a vast fortune, had followed his heart and pursued his dream of becoming a physician. Ewan P. Gallagher had a different dream. Acting in local theater, the talented twenty-year-old was determined to be a famous success.

As fate would have it, Jason happened to be working in

casualty one night when Ewan was admitted as a patient. Jason was more than flattered and surprisingly aroused by the younger man's obvious attraction to him. The two men entered into a steamy affair finding love, until their ambitions pulled them apart.

Now, one year later and stuck in a sham of a marriage that he entered into only to preserve his inheritance, Jason is filled with regret. Caught between obligation and freedom, duty and desire, Jason finds that he can no longer deny his passion. He plans to win Ewan, Hollywood's newest rising star, back!

The G.A. Hauser Collection

Unnecessary Roughness

Got Men?

Heart of Steele

All Man

Hot Rod

London, Bloody, London

Julian

Black Leather Phoenix

In The Dark and What Should Never Be, Erotic Short Stories

Mark and Sharon (formally titled A Question of Sex)

A Man's Best Friend

It Takes a Man

The Physician and the Actor

For Love and Money

The Kiss

Naked Dragon

Secrets and Misdemeanors

Capital Games

Giving Up the Ghost

To Have and To Hostage

Love you, Loveday

The Boy Next Door

When Adam Met Jack

Exposure

The Vampire and the Man-eater

Murphy's Hero

Mark Antonious deMontford

Prince of Servitude

Calling Dr Love

The Rape of St. Peter

The Wedding Planner

Going Deep

Double Trouble

Pirates

Miller's Tale

Vampire Nights

Teacher's Pet

In the Shadow of Alexander

The Rise and Fall of the Sacred Band of Thebes

The Action Series

Acting Naughty

Playing Dirty

Getting it in the End

Behaving Badly

Dripping Hot

Packing Heat

Being Screwed

Men in Motion Series

Mile High

Cruising

Driving Hard

Leather Boys

Heroes Series

Man to Man

Two In Two Out

Top Men

G.A. Hauser

Writing as Amanda Winters

Sister Moonshine

14313954R00124

Made in the USA
Lexington, KY
21 March 2012